The Last
of the
Roundup
Boys

The Last
of the
Roundup
Boys

by
Debra Seely

Holiday House/*New York*

Acknowledgments

For all their help with the writing of this book I'd like to thank my parents, the Milton Center Writer's Workshop, Lois Ruby, Dian Curtis Regan, Clare Vanderpool, Erin McGraw, Regina Griffin, the Glen Workshop, Ron Ryan, Rusty Smoker, Rita Sevart, and Dave, Michael, Elise, and Matthew Seely.

Library of Congress Cataloging-in-Publication Data
Seely, Debra.
The last of the roundup boys / Debra Seely.—1st ed.
p. cm.
Summary: In 1886 in Kansas, seventeen-year-old Tom,
the son of a poor farmer, is hired as a cowboy on a cattle ranch
and faces the challenges of both herding work
and a forbidden romance with sixteen-year-old Evie,
the ranch owner's independently-minded daughter.
ISBN 0-8234-1814-6 (hardcover)
[1. Cowboys—Fiction. 2. Sex role—Fiction.
3. Coming of age—Fiction. 4. Ranch life—Kansas—Fiction.
5. Kansas—History—19th century—Fiction.] I. Title.
PZ7.S4518Las 2004
[Fic]—dc22   2003056754

For my great-grandparents

Contents

The Last
of the
Roundup
Boys

I.
Traplines
Tom

∾o∾

When Grandmother died of influenza in November, Grandfather was already sick, and he died a few days later. My sister, Becky, wired, begging me to come home for their funeral. The telegraph operator rode his pony all the way from the train station one night to deliver the cable. He pounded on the log door, scaring us because night visitors never brought good news. Papa opened the door and took the yellow sheets. I watched his face as he read and knew what the wire said even before he handed me one of the papers. DIED PEACEFULLY. A BLESSING THEY ARE IN HEAVEN TOGETHER. THEY MISSED YOU. GRANDFATHER'S LAST THOUGHTS OF YOU, TOM. HIS DEAREST WISH THAT YOU RETURN.

How I would return, and to whom, or what, Becky didn't say. She was preoccupied with her life as a married woman in Norfolk. She never mentioned sending money for a train ticket.

Of course money was why I didn't return for the funeral, even though I'd wanted to, even though I'd run out in the cold and dark to the buffalo wallow behind the barn to cry where no one could see me. Cry hard, too, like a baby cries, like my lungs and heart would sob themselves out of my chest. Dust and tears caked my face. I surprised myself crying that way, old as I was. I felt guilty for leaving to live with my father, guilty for not returning to two people who had loved me the best they knew how, who'd raised me after my mother died. How much they'd loved me I was only beginning to see, by comparing it to what I had at my father's.

I'd come to be a cowboy but had stayed to become part of my father's new family. Kansas had been tough. We'd sold our calves the fall before, put most of the money into seed wheat and fence, then lost the summer's wheat crop and had to sell the cattle, keeping only a cow. The garden didn't grow during the summer because of the drought. The corn crop yielded all right, a twenty-acre field in good bottom land next to the creek, except that my papa had planted half of it in wheat, which he lost. We had corn mush for breakfast, corn bread for dinner, corn pudding for supper, and little else.

Plenty of sickness, though, when fall came, and doctor bills, because my stepbrother and stepsister couldn't fight off anything after their bout with whooping cough. I couldn't go to the high school in town, because I had to stay on the farm and help with the planting, a job that was beginning to seem increasingly useless. In fact, I hadn't been to school for one reason or another since I was thirteen and had come west. I'd given up pretending that my education was temporarily waylaid. I wasn't ever going back.

Being seventeen in and of itself made me an easy target for my folks' rage in these tough times. Of course, they tried not to take their anger out on me. I had become a hard worker, good in the fields, good with the livestock, satisfied with the contribution I was making, and both my papa and Mattie respected that contribution. The day before the telegram came, Papa, after supper, had asked my advice about planting for spring and hinted that I might work one of the fields by myself, getting

ready for the day when I'd have my own fields. I'd
swelled with pride, then sobered when he said that
day was a long way off. But the thought remained.

Mattie noticed my soberness, and said, "You've
grown a foot overnight, I swear. No wonder your
father's thinking you're ready for your own fields.
Those pants will never do. Come over here and let
me measure you, so I can fix up some pants of your
father's to fit." She set about doing for me without the complaints she used to make when I first
arrived. I had grown, not tall, but overnight all
my clothes were too small. I had thick-muscled
arms, work-hardened hands, and thighs strong as
fence posts. Uneasy in this new body, I tripped over
the rag rug, knocking over her sewing basket. I
helped her put the thread and scissors back and
picked up the pins off the wood floor. "Make sure
you get every last pin—don't want them wasted
and don't want no one getting stuck in the foot,"
she said, and her voice held a tightness that said
she was holding back her irritation.

You never want to think that someone who
cares for you would do something that was unfair
to you, even if it was for your own good, in the long
run. Of course, I didn't think about the word *love*
in connection with my father—I suppose I loved

him, and he me, in his way, but it wasn't anything we ever talked about. We just knew it was there, which made what happened next bitter for me to swallow.

The day after the telegram came, long before the rest of us were up, Mattie and my father hitched the team to the wagon and headed down the new graded road to town, leaving us three children to run the place by ourselves. This was the first time they'd driven away together without us, and we wondered what they were up to. "You don't think they'll sell the place, do you, Tom?" Caleb asked me anxiously as we did our morning barn chores. Caleb was thirteen now and could do the work as fast as I could, no longer trying to compete with me like he used to. "Abner Wurtz's papa and mama sold out. They all went west to Idaho, and I never saw him again."

I paused. I should have been with my folks going to town, to wire Becky, to talk with my papa about going back for the funeral, to talk about memories, doing something to acknowledge my grandparents' passing. My eyes followed the road the folks had taken, running in a straight line across the pasture a mile to the east, where it intersected with another new road that ran due south to town. "I think if they were going to sell they'd tell us," I said, not at all sure they would. In fact, all of a sudden I wondered if Caleb was right. I forced myself to focus on him. "Would Idaho be so bad?" I asked.

"I don't know nobody lives in Idaho except Abner," Caleb declared, "and even though he took my slingshot with him, I wouldn't go there just to collect. He said it snows so high it buries the houses." Caleb pondered this, getting interested. "And there's mountains. You figure we'd get stuck in a snowdrift on some mountain and have to eat each other, like them people in California?"

He meant the Donner party, whose ghosts got resurrected in the gossip at the general store every time someone lost his farm and headed west in the fall. It wasn't pleasant to think of, grieving as I was, especially with our bellies so empty and winter coming on. "You wouldn't be more than a mouthful anyway," I said, tossing some straw at him.

"You think it'd be right to do something like that, eat human flesh, to save your life?"

I thought about this, eyeing him, not knowing how serious he was. "Would you do it?"

"I don't know. Maybe. Look at it this way. If you was starving, and I was already dead, what difference would it make to me? You could take a little bite out of me, and I'd never know."

"Well, thank you. I'll keep that in mind."

"I guess that would make it right, if it helped save someone."

"I don't know as I'd like part of me being cut away, without me knowing," I said.

"You wouldn't make more than two mouthfuls anyway," Caleb said, and he tossed straw back at me.

He was probably right. But it wasn't funny, talking about hunger when you're hungry, so we let it drop till noon, then headed toward the house. Emma, at twelve was already a good farm woman, making the most of scarcity. But today she had set out only three boiled potatoes.

"I looked down in the cellar and in the cupboards," she announced, "and there ain't no more but a bushel of potatoes. The cornmeal is all gone, Thomas. I don't know how Mama expects me to feed you today. I'll milk tonight, and we can eat eggs this evening after the hens lay, but no bread to eat 'em with. There's some pumpkins, but no sugar or flour for a pie."

"Let's go fishin'!" Caleb piped up. "A mess of catfish would taste awful good just now."

"You can't go anywhere in this cold without a coat, much less fishing all afternoon," I said. "You'd catch your death all over again, and not be able to look at a fish, much less taste it. I'll go check the lines this afternoon."

Papa and Caleb and I kept lines baited in a fishing hole at the creek, about a mile from the house. Usually, fishing was good only in summer, when the fish were active and straining at insects above the water. In cold weather they went to the creek bottom, and we rarely caught anything. But we always tried. We also set traplines at points about a mile further along the creek for the scarce small game—rabbits, beavers, squirrels—around the country. Most of the time the lines did not yield anything, and that was my luck when I rode my horse, Wanderer, out to check. I put fresh bait on the hooks and in the traps, and after I'd finished with the last one I sat down and let my eyes drift, along the creek, over the prairie. This part of the township hadn't been graded yet, and the prairie was still like it had been, free to roam. But far to the south, where before there had been only grass, three houses now sprouted up, forming a triangle a mile wide. I didn't know who lived in them.

Tom

I hadn't thought about going back to Virginia since making up my mind to stay in Kansas four years ago. Even though life was harder than I'd imagined, I was glad to know my father, glad to be in a place where I was needed. I'd written faithfully to my grandparents and sister, and they'd kept wanting me to come back, but I'd grown into this place more every year. In the summers, I used to graze the herd along this creek. As the country filled up, other boys would bring their herds here to graze and drink, and we used to swim and splash as the sun shone on the water and the cattle wandered. I'd made friends to replace my Virginia schoolyard gang. Some would last only a summer or two and then move on with their families, but others, from the Mennonite settlement and from the Methodist settlement, stuck around. I hadn't seen them much since we'd sold the cattle. Their families, like most farmers lately, had fenced their cattle anyway. Herding days were passing, although the big ranches to the west of us still grazed the open range. But the boys were busy like me, helping their families and getting ready to farm on their own someday. I thought about riding over to visit the Mennonites, a few miles distant, but the wind took on a fiercer chill, and I headed back to the cabin.

About suppertime we saw Papa and Mattie driving back in the wagon. Its back end was loaded down. We helped unhitch, and then unloaded a feast—barrels of salt pork, sacks of flour, salt, cornmeal, dried beans, jars of molasses. Our stomachs rumbled at the sight of so much. Then there were skeins of colored yarn done up in brown paper, and a bolt of wool fabric.

"You'll need a winter coat," Mattie said to me as we unloaded the wool. "You'll have to pass your outgrown coat to Caleb for this winter."

My grandparents had sent me a fine tailored wool coat last year. They must have remembered me as a smaller boy, for I outgrew the coat in two months, but I kept wearing it, having no alternative. Plus, it reminded me of nice Virginia things—the fabric was finely woven, the buttons brass. It still looked like new, and even though I was glad to be getting a coat that fit, it would be a coarse, homemade one, unlike the one that would now be Caleb's, and this soured the deal.

The big question, of course, the one we were afraid of, was how they paid for all this plenty. Papa was already in debt for next year's seed wheat. "I sold something," Papa said, avoiding my eyes. The plow, my horse and saddle, the cow, were all still here. I'd read about sacrifices—selling precious heirlooms, watches, silver—to escape dire straits. But our spare log house was stripped of ornaments, and Mattie and Papa of all but the necessaries. Anything of value must have been sold long ago, before they'd met. There was nothing decorative from Mattie's former life, nothing left of my mother's.

"You sold the farm." I didn't ask him, just said it flat out.

Papa turned to face me. "Whatever else I have to do, I'll hang on to this farm. I put too much into it to give it up now."

"What then?"

"Never you mind." But he didn't look at me as he said this.

We had a week of eating like railroad barons. On top of the bounty from the store, we had a prize—a deer Papa shot on a fishing trip a few days after he'd been to town. Although Papa always carried a shotgun out on the prairie, we never hunted. There was not much game around anymore, not like there had been when Papa first came out here. Deer had been scarce for several years. So this deer we skinned and cleaned carefully, smoked the two hams, pounded jerky, dried the hide to tan for leather, and ate all we could of the rest, because it wouldn't keep.

The night he shot the deer, Papa gave me the choicest cut of the venison steaks. Usually, the one who made the kill got the choice part, or the extra parts, if there were any.

"You take it," I said.

"Go on," he replied. "You're growing."

I didn't want to argue, so I helped myself to the sweet red meat. Papa had sizzled it over an open fire pit, the way the cowboys did, and its richness melted on my tongue, its warmth more than making up for past empty bellies.

We didn't talk, as usual, at supper. Everyone concentrated on the steaks and the pumpkin pie Mattie had made. After dinner, though, there was none of the hurry-up to finish chores. For once we felt so full we couldn't move. We bundled up and took our stools outside and sat in the yard, watching the pit fire burn down. The evening was crisp, the stars clear.

Papa began to talk of plans. "We'll breed the milk cow next week, although she may be past her rut. Have to pay Weinhardt for the bull's service again. Thought I'd have my own bull by now. I'll pay cash, not kind, so we can keep the calf to sell." Again I thought to ask him where the cash would come from, but the peace of the night sky made me indisposed to spoil the evening.

The next week Papa sent me to the Weinhardt place to fetch the bull. In the four years since their daughter Marie's death on the prairie, Mr. and Mrs. Weinhardt had aged more than ten, with gray streaking their hair and lines creasing their faces. There was a brittleness about their family, as if they moved carefully to avoid breaking. I wondered if my family appeared that way to outsiders, ever since my baby half brother Jacob died.

They invited me up to the porch to sit, and Mrs. Weinhardt brought out glasses of water and fresh-baked cinnamon bread. "I'm sorry to hear about your grandparents," Mrs. Weinhardt said.

I lowered my eyes, not able to say anything.

"Didn't think to see you for several weeks," said Mr. Weinhardt.

"Why not?" I asked.

"Thought you went back to Virginia, for the funeral. We hear that you was going."

"I didn't have money to go back," I said.

"Ach, the gossip in this place. We hear they send you money. But I hear more than once that I sell my farm and move back to Strasbourg—news to me, and more so to my wife, I'm sure."

"Who told you they sent me money?"

"The telegram man, he tells me this when I'm at the train station the other day. What does he know, anyway? He should stay out of other people's business."

At the bull pen, I watched him clip a lead rope through the bull's nose ring. With the ring, the bull followed me home placidly enough. I put him in the empty corral. They were all in the big room eating dinner. I walked past them without a word, went straight to my father's bedroom, and took his business ledger from his trunk.

Sometimes, checking my traplines, I'd be horrified by what the steel jaws had snared. Once I found a beaver leg twisted in the metal teeth, with the white of the bone sticking through the bloody flesh, the blood darkening the brown fur into matted clumps. I don't know if the horror came from the leg itself or the thought of the beaver without it.

The same shock flooded me when I pulled the ledger book out of my father's trunk and a bank receipt floated out of it. My name stared up at me from the floor, like the dead eyes of a trapped animal. *To Thomas Hunter in receipt of check, sum of one hundred dollars, paid cash in full to legal representative, Joseph Hunter, father.* Dated the day Mattie and my father went to town for the supplies.

I stormed into the big room. "You took it! She did send money for a train ticket, for the funeral! My money!" I held the paper under his nose, threw the ledger to the floor.

"Be sensible. By the time you'd have got there, the funeral would have been over with."

"What's this money then?"

Papa's eyes, when he finally looked at me, were still as stone. "Money Becky wired for a ticket," he said quietly. "A one-way ticket."

"You had no right!" I moaned, sinking onto the army cot, feeling sick at my stomach. "You had no right."

2.
Punishment
Tom

⚬⚬⚬

The next day I didn't get up for chores and my father threatened to whip me. At dinner Mattie complained about a rip I'd put in my newly made-over trousers. She snapped at my extra helping of fried rabbit. Papa, as usual, didn't say much, but he didn't look at me either. In fact, he avoided my eyes. I suppose that's what made me take a big bite out of that piece of rabbit right in front of Mattie as she stood there yelling. I wasn't all that hungry, hadn't been since the night before. But I sat there glaring at her as I ate the forbidden food.

Suddenly she snatched the plate away. I grabbed for it, knocking her forearm hard, and she smacked me across the cheek with her free hand.

I couldn't believe she'd hit me, as many times as she had threatened. I jumped up, knocking over my chair, then grabbed her arm and twisted it behind her back. I was as tall as she was now, and stronger. "Don't ever touch me again," I said, "or I'll break your arm, I swear it."

"Thomas!" Papa's voice cut into my rage, and I let go of Mattie's arm. She sagged back, away from me, pale, but her eyes were blazing. Papa lunged for me, pinning my arms. I struggled to get free, but he was too strong for me. "You are never to touch her that way, you hear me? Never."

"She hit me!" I yelled.

He let go and gave me a shove. "Get outside!" he thundered. "To the corncrib."

I stormed out the door. In the yard, I heard their voices, yelling, and then Papa's voice saying, "We've made it bad enough already," but I didn't stop to listen. I headed for the barn, saddled Wanderer, and headed out for the open prairie.

All afternoon I rode hard. By evening I was at the Chikaskia River, near one of the spots I'd camped when bringing the cattle home after the Parsons herd stampeded them. The grass was high here, and the land level and empty still. I dismounted and let Wanderer graze. The sky turned orange and streaks of clouds in the west glowed gold. The light on the water made a golden river. Then the sun sank lower, and the gold river became ordinary again, and gray. My old cowboy dreams seemed like they belonged to someone else now. The cattle were gone, sold or butchered to keep us from starving. There never had been money to finish the fence for them anyhow.

But I wasn't going back to be locked in a corn-crib. Maybe that's how they could treat the children, but I was grown now.

It was too cold to get comfortable, even with a dung fire. Always carrying matches was a holdover from the herding days, when we'd build campfires to roast the catfish we caught. I still carried hook and line too, but there wasn't much point in fishing, even though I was hungry. The starlight glittered as though nail holes were punched in the cold black sky. November in Kansas rarely brought snow, but the frost chilled. I hadn't brought my coat, in my hurry, and I shivered, with only the horse's saddle blanket under me and a cover of the thin blanket I kept strapped to my saddle.

I would run off to Montana. Maybe I'd find Luke, who'd left the Parsons ranch three years ago, after the stampede. And then I realized I was going to have to go back home in the morning. Much as I wanted to run away, it was no use at this time of year. Fall roundups were over; no ranchers would be hiring, and no farmers would need workers either. Even running off to Montana or Texas would have to wait until spring, when the weather would let me travel and the ranchers would be starting the cattle on the trails. I could try a railroad crew, but even in their greedy push across the country, the railroads didn't hire much in winter.

So I lay on the cold ground and thought about where to go in the spring, and then about surviving at home until then, a much less enjoyable prospect, and at last the dawn broke and I got up, limping from my night outside.

My father said nothing as I rode in and stabled my horse, then went about my chores as usual. Only the strain in the silence was different. But midmorning, I found that Wanderer was gone, and so was the big bay. I ran to the house. Papa was nowhere around.

"Where is he?" I demanded of Mattie. She was rolling dough and barely glanced at me.

"Don't know," she said, and when I kept standing there, glaring at her, she snapped, "You expect he tells me every little thing?"

She was lying so obviously I wanted to shake her.

Long after dark, I heard hoofbeats from the west and ran out to meet him. He was riding on the bay and leading my horse. "What did you do?" I yelled.

"Found you a job."

This was so far from what I was expecting that I didn't know what to say. He rode to the barn and I followed. "What were you doing with my horse?"

Papa turned to face me. "Let's get one thing straight," he said. "This farm, and everything that goes with it, is mine, to do with as I see fit."

"Not my horse. He was a gift to me."

"Including your horse. He sleeps in my barn and eats my grass. If I want to sell him, that's my right. And that's what I intended to do this morning."

"No!"

Papa held up his hand to shush me. "As I said, I intended to. Can't have you riding off every time you have a fit, and I thought he'd bring a good price from Parsons. That's where I went. But, turns out he recognized this horse. Said he didn't want it, it was the stubbornest thing he'd ever come across. Only one cowboy could ride it, his old foreman. Must have meant that cowboy that give it to you, what was his name?"

Luke, I thought. But I didn't give him the satisfaction of answering.

"Anyway, I told him that must be why it got along with my son—he's just as stubborn." Papa squinted at me here, but I didn't say anything. "I told him you could ride him all right, there wasn't nothing wrong with him.

"Then he gets interested, asks me how old you are now, and what you're up to. Turns out his cowhands have pneumonia. He needs someone to help out, for the time. Well, ordinarily, I wouldn't want you working for that man. He'd like to see us fail, so he could have the land. I don't know as I trust his offer." My father looked at me squarely. He knew I felt the same way about Parsons. He looked away as he spoke again, so low I almost couldn't hear him. "But the fact is, son, we got to get money from somewhere or we won't make it. You're to show up for work there tomorrow."

Was he telling me to leave? "The Parsons place is too far to ride back and forth," I said. We both knew what I meant.

"You'll stay at the bunkhouse on the place. Just until his men get well."

For the first time in I don't know how many months, my father's orders didn't chafe at me. But I couldn't let him know that. "And if I say no?"

"You do what *I* say."

3.
A Cowboy Career
Tom

Until the Parsons place, no human construction I'd seen in the West had looked permanent. Everything was sod or wood, slapped up, less than a dozen years old, and if a tornado or even a stiff wind came along, it would all be flattened in seconds. But the Parsons place was built to stay. This was one of the few two-story houses I'd come across, made of a dark lumber I'd never seen before. A gabled attic story topped it, and an unusual porch with a claylike arch fronted it. A real yard, instead of a dirt area, skirted the front of the house, with planted elm trees more than a dozen feet tall, big enough to give some shade in summer. A wooden swing hung from a low branch of the tallest tree.

I rode down the dirt lane slowly, sizing up what I was getting into. Behind the trees, farther down the lane and to the left, stood the bunkhouse, a low wooden building about like our cabin, and, looming over all, a long wooden barn, giant, made of the same dark planks as the house. A roomy chicken coop, storage crib, and hog shed lay behind the house to the right. All in all, the Parsons place was handsome—maybe oversized, but not so much grand as solid and practical.

The view from the house looking southwest stopped me. The land rolled away for miles, covered with shaggy yellow grass that rippled down to a thick, wandering line of bare trees maybe five miles distant. Beyond those trees, which bordered the Chikaskia River, the land swelled into gentle ridges and blue bluffs easing into the low edges of the sky. It was rough country, yet its openness beckoned.

The sun wasn't yet overhead. I had gotten away from my father's place early as possible, after breakfast and chores. I left my trunk, but put my clothes and a razor in an old feed sack, along with my journal and a few books. I took two slices of buttered bread for a noon meal, not wanting to impose on the house to feed me right away. I came from the east on the new road that ran from town a mile south of my father's and directly past the Parsons place, about five miles from ours.

No one was around. I tied Wanderer to a tree at the back and knocked on the kitchen door. A tiny lady in a huge white apron opened it immediately. "Yes?"

She had a slight German accent. I thought she must have been the cook. "I'm Thomas Hunter— here to see Mr. Parsons about a job as a cowhand?"

Her brief glance took me in from head to toe and then some. She laughed, and the edges of her eyes crinkled. "I thought as much from your getup."

I blushed at this. Remembering the cowboys from the stampede, I'd put on a bandanna and braided a leather band around my hat, which was pulled low.

"Well, we're pleased to have you, cowboy. Mr. Parsons is in town for the day. Take your horse to the stable and your bag to the bunkhouse. There is an empty bunk there you can store your things under. Then you come back and help me. I'm running a hospital these days, what with the sick hired men. Go, hurry. Wash your hands when you come back."

This wasn't the start I had envisioned for my cowboy career, but I did as she said, feeling it best not to cross her. The stable—an extra wing of the barn, with stalls and a tack room—was warm, but the bunkhouse was icy. Dusty too—it made me sneeze. To my surprise, though, there were no sick cowboys in it. The room, about the size of the big room at home, was empty. There were three unused beds, two chests, a table and chairs, a stand with a bowl and empty pitcher, and an unlit coal stove. I gulped my bread, stuffed the sack under a bunk, and hurried back to the house.

I knocked awhile, but no one came, so I pulled the door open and stepped inside. Smells of chicken soup and liniment hit me as I entered the kitchen, a large, airy room gleaming with brass. The cook was nowhere in sight, nor was anyone else. I caught myself tiptoeing down the long oak hallway, and then it dawned on me that I was afraid to run into Evie Parsons.

Now, I had run into Evie dozens of times out on the prairie, although less after she started high school, and had never been afraid of meeting her. In fact, I kind of looked forward to it, because she always had something interesting to say, and her hair was somewhat nice-looking. I hadn't seen her for more than a year, probably, but why I should be afraid to meet her in her own house I didn't know. My breathing became irregular, all the same.

So when I saw her at the writing desk in the parlor, it was like someone hit me in the stomach. She sat bent over the desk, reading, and the gray light from the window gave her long copper curls a pearly glow. I just stood there, like a dolt, as she looked up from her book.

"Criminy! Don't scare me like that! What are you doing here, anyhow?" she said.

I managed to draw myself up, attempting to look like a person who was now employed. "I'm working for your father. Just got here. I'm supposed to be helping the cook, only I can't find her."

"That's because we haven't got a cook."

I felt myself start to blush, and was furious at my give-away blood vessels. "The lady with the German accent?"

She laughed. "That's my mother!"

Well, there was no more worry about making myself look stupid now. I stood there awkwardly, until I noticed what she was working on. "You're reading *Huckleberry Finn* at school?" I envied her attending a school that would assign such a new, irreverent novel.

But now she blushed. "Old Tyler, my English teacher, wouldn't call this literature. I told Mama it was for school, because she'd never let me read it otherwise. You know it?"

"I do." It lay in my sack in the bunkhouse as we spoke. I had traded one of the books my grandfather sent me for it at the general store, one of only two books on display there, the other being *Principles of Animal Husbandry.*

"Evie Parsons! Back to that book. And you, young man"—Mrs. Parsons stood in the doorway, eyeing me accusingly now—"out. Evie has to study. Take these sheets to the basement and fill the copper tub with water for washing." She pointed to a pile in the hallway. "Get moving."

Surprised at the change in her manner, I backed away, knocked the heel of my boot against the doorway molding, and stumbled down the hall. From one bossy woman to another.

The sheets stunk and suspicious colored stains spotted them. I carried them none too close. I wished Evie hadn't been there.

At noon my chore was to carry chicken soup upstairs to the cowboys, and this meant going back through the parlor. Luckily Evie had left, and I was spared the humiliation of looking like a clumsy waiter. The double staircase curving up from the back of the parlor was wide and made of cherry wood. It ran to either side of a fireplace big enough to roast a pig in, topped with a fancy cherry wood mantel carved with all sorts of curlicues. An unlit crystal chandelier hung overhead in the middle of the parlor. The walls were papered with an elaborate design I hadn't seen even in Virginia.

On the second floor, doors with crystal doorknobs lined the hallways that stretched to my right and in front of me, making an L-shape. In a back bedroom, off the foot of the L, two gaunt men, whom I nevertheless recognized from the cattle stampede as Shorty and Lightning Jack, lay stretched across cots put up in what looked like a guest room. The feather bed, lofty with down and covered with a bright quilt and snowy pillows, sat untouched; the cots crowded at the foot of it. At least the room was warmer than the bunkhouse.

The two of them lay side by side on the cots. Back where I'd grown up, my grandparents would never have put a colored man in a sickroom with a white man.

The cowboys were asleep and snoring, so I tiptoed in and set the bowls beside them, then tiptoed back out, feeling like a boy in a fairy tale who tries not to wake the slumbering giant.

I expected to be served by myself in the kitchen, but when Mrs. Parsons called, "Dinner!" Evie arrived there, and we three sat down to eat together. Mrs. Parsons was friendly again as she passed mashed potatoes and fried catfish, bread and butter, and canned beets from a quart jar. I tried to act like such a feast was normal, but still took too much and ate too fast. Mrs. Parsons was picky about Evie's table manners, telling her several times to keep her elbows off the table, use her napkin, and not shovel food into her mouth. I had to remind myself to do the same, especially to use the cloth napkin, which I'd not seen on a table since leaving Virginia, but Mrs. Parsons seemed not to mind any lapses on my part.

"You must have noticed we have Shorty, our colored cowboy, in the house same as our white one," Mrs. Parsons said to me. "They are where the inside help usually sleeps. But we have no inside help now. They need to be kept warm, out of that drafty bunkhouse, and it's easier to take care of both of them when they're together." She raised her eyebrows to show that there was to be no argument on this point. I nodded.

"Mr. Parsons and the other children will be home at supper," Mrs. Parsons said. "Thomas, you'll join us for meals, and you're welcome to spend this evening with us in the parlor. We don't do anything fancy, but if Evie's finished her studies, she can pop some corn for us. And join us for services in the parlor tomorrow morning. We live too far to get to town for church regularly, but we hold our own worship, and we like for the help to come."

"Thank you, ma'am." I'd forgotten about Sundays. My family ignored them, treating every day much the same as any other.

"Then we'll leave to take Evie and Chester back to town, for school. You'll look after the hired men while we're away."

"Yes ma'am."

"Back to the warden," Evie said, making a face.

"Evelyn Marie! Shame on that talk! Miss Watkins is more than kind to let you stay with her during the week. Poor woman, with no one in town to take care of her, she has more than her share of struggles."

"She causes me more than my share." Evie glanced at me and giggled. "Last week Hazel Wilson came over, and I played a new song on the piano for her about a girl who runs away with a peddler. Miss Watkins had a fit. Said it wasn't proper for ladies to be singing about such things, and she made Hazel go home. She has this vein above her eyebrow that bulges when she gets mad, and it was about to blow. The rest of the week, when she was around, I'd hum the tune real low, like I wasn't paying attention, and that old vein would just pop right out."

"What song is that?" Mrs. Parsons looked quizzically at her daughter. "I don't know that one. It don't sound too proper to me, either."

Evie stopped chewing. She'd said too much, that was plain. "Oh, it's just one everyone at school knows."

"Everyone but Hazel Wilson, yes? Evie, if you've been running around where you shouldn't, your father will thrash you."

"No, Mama, you can ask Miss Watkins. I don't go out during the week, I swear."

"You know there's a rough element in town, even with that beer hall closed, and you know you best keep away from it. You help me with these dishes now."

"Yes ma'am." But as her mother stood and

turned toward the sink, Evie kicked me under the table and mouthed the words, *I'll tell you later.*

I started to help clear the table, not able to keep from noticing how good she smelled, and how the dress she wore made her look grown up. I'd never seen her in anything but her tied-up riding skirt before. Then Mrs. Parsons planted herself between us and, her voice harsh again, ordered me to fetch the dishes from the sickroom.

I wondered if Evie really did run around town at night, in the rough places.

4.
Women's Work
Tom

Nursemaid chores for Mrs. Parsons kept me busy all afternoon, until I was mightily sick of them. But one good thing came of them: Evie found me in the basement, hanging bedsheets up to dry on the line. It was clear that she wasn't supposed to be there by the way she sneaked down the stairs, looking over her shoulder. She saw me watching her and smiled.

"You must think I'm pretty bad," she said.

"No more than usual. But just how does a girl go about picking up songs that upset her mama?"

She looked at me hard. "Promise you won't tell?"

"Promise."

"Well. I don't sneak out. Really. Only I did, this one time. They said at school that there was a woman speaker coming to town hall in the evening. It was so easy to get away from Miss Watkins, I really should do it more often. I just told her I was studying with Hazel, and Hazel came to get me, and we went to the town hall. This woman speaker talked about the problems the railroads created for the farmers, and how farmers should band together, even how women should vote. That's why I wanted to hear her. I think women should vote too. They do in Wyoming, you know."

"You're not old enough to vote."

"Neither are you. That doesn't mean I shouldn't when I am old enough. Anyway, I caught sight of Papa. He was about to have a stroke, because she lumped the cattlemen and the railroads together and called them enemies of farmers. Seeing me in that crowd of rowdies would have finished him off. So, I had to hide. I ducked into the blacksmith's. There was this cowboy there getting a wagon wheel banded and he was drunk, and sang this song over and over. Then he tried to give me a kiss, but the blacksmith yelled at him and I pushed him away and ran off. I'd lost Hazel by this time, and didn't see my father anywhere, so I just went back to Miss Watkins's house. That's all there was to it."

"I would have punched him for you," I said.

"Mighty chivalrous of you. But I can handle his type."

Looking at her, I had no doubt that she could.

"So, you finished your 'schoolwork'?" I teased.

She made a face. "I'm not very free around here, Tom. You'll see that for yourself soon enough." She settled on the bottom step of the stairs. "If I'm not doing homework or chores for Mama, I'm set to embroider. Pillowcases, mostly, for my hope chest, for when they can marry me off to someone else I'll have to do for. 'Idle hands are the devil's playthings,' that's Mama's motto. I have to pretend to study so I can read, otherwise Mama thinks I'm wasting time. I'm free only when I read or ride the prairie."

That sounded familiar enough. "My stepmother thinks reading is a waste of time too," I said. "I used to sneak books out to read while I was herding."

"I wish I could go out herding," she said. "I could never do that, even after I bought my own cow. I'm building a herd, you know. It's about five head now is all, but it's mine. Only you think Papa will let me ride with you to take care of it? Of course not." She sighed. "Might as well put it in my hope chest too, for all the good it does me."

"I wouldn't want a whiff of that chest," I said, and she laughed. "I remember, years ago, when we'd go out bone collecting, you always said you'd buy a cow with the money, and now you've got five. We've sold most of our herd. The corn crop failed, and we needed the money. Seems like the only ones around here who prosper are like your papa, the ones who already have the most." A bitterness crept into my voice as I spoke.

"You sound like that woman speaker." She watched me pin up bedding for a time. "You don't like us, do you?" she said at last.

I took my time searching for a clothespin in the basket, looking for one without a chip in the carved wood. "It's not whether I like you or not," I said. "Things would just be better for my folks— for all of us—if we had some of what you have. Anyways, I'd rather be working my own place. My very own place, not my papa's or your papa's."

I hadn't known this until I heard myself say the words, but I knew it was true. She sat quiet a long time. I finished hauling up a wet bedsheet and glanced at her. She was watching me with eyes that made me want to drown all of a sudden. I became aware that I was sopping wet, letting her stare at me while I did women's work. I looked down, uncomfortable at not being able to walk away.

"Why doesn't your mother have a hired girl to do this?" I asked.

She shrugged. "Mama said the last one disgraced herself. I was at school and no one would tell me more."

She must have guessed that I was embarrassed, because she said, "I'd best get busy," and stood to go upstairs. "Did you know there's a tunnel to the barn?" she said suddenly.

"Show me," I said.

But her mother called for her. "I will, soon enough," she whispered, and ran upstairs.

5.
A Narrow Escape
Tom

I had to take supper to the sick men. I heard the coughing as I entered the room.

They recognized me, even though it had been four years. "Well, if it ain't the boy we nearly trampled to death," Lightning Jack said, raising himself up to sit.

"You lose your cows again?" Shorty asked. "You ain't gonna find 'em up here, though I swear, all this hacking is liable to be took for cattle-bellowing." He stopped, overtaken by coughing.

"Shorty's so noisy over there I can't get my beauty sleep," Lightning Jack said.

"That must be the truth, 'cause you sorely need some beauty," Shorty retorted.

"Well, you can take all the time you need to rest up, now that I'm here," I said. "I'll be looking after things till you're well."

Lightning Jack snorted. "And that's supposed to make us feel better?"

"Just leave everything to me." A teacup fell off the stack I was clearing, and I held my breath until it hit the soft carpet rug, unharmed but sloshing a nasty liquid onto the floor.

"Oh Lordy," Shorty breathed as I mopped it up. "Please let us get well soon. Good thing this is the slow time of year. Not much to do, Tom, but look after the stock that's around the house—the horses and the milk cows." He stopped to cough and spit green phlegm into a bowl under his cot. "Mr. Parsons and Chester—that's his boy—they like to take care of the buggies themselves, but you look after the wagon. Check fences some, and mend some saddles—no, you leave them saddles to me."

"We're 'bout to go stark crazy up here with nothin' to do but cough," Lightning Jack complained. "Soon's we're up and about, we're ridin' hell for leather to town, to one a them drugstores, and get the real cure, yessir. You ever been to a drugstore?"

I had, when the family went to town. It was a regular store, as far as I could tell, with shelves of brightly colored medicine bottles in the front windows and display counters with tweezers, gauze, liniment, bag balm, tooth pincers—no place I'd want to go *after* I'd been sick.

Jack laughed. "You ever go 'round to the back door? After the danged fools in Topeka put the saloons out of business a few years back, a man had to go somewhere to wet his whistle, and durned if them druggists didn't cook up the right medicine! There's more drugstores now than sick people."

"They ain't nowhere like the saloons was, though," Shorty complained. "They act all sneaky-like and you can't drink in 'em, just buy your whiskey and go, and some of 'em won't sell to me at all."

"I'll buy you more'n you and me could drink in a week, with a drop left over for Tom here." Jack looked up at me. "You old enough to down the demon rum by now, boy? High time we was corruptin' you. How are you at cards? There's still some good poker games to be had. Say, if you can sneak a deck past the missus, we can do some of our own business right up here. She sure don't hold with card playin'."

"You goin' to get him run out of here before he even gets started," Shorty said. "You best leave off, Jack."

They asked after my family, and I answered as briefly as possible, then turned the talk to how they got sick in the first place. "Well, now, there's a tale," Jack said. "There's a good place to ford the Chikaskia, about five miles west of here, south some. We was across it heading home, after we'd drove some heifers up to winter range the other side of the river. Well, that river is only two feet at its deepest, and there's no quicksand at the ford, so we wasn't particularly lookin' out for trouble. We was hungry, and I'm tellin' Shorty about some food made by this chuck-wagon cook I knowed from Texas years ago, this colored cowpoke name of Lefler, who is a barber in San Antone now. He made the best biscuits in creation and could do wonders with shoe leather if he had to.

"And I start tellin' Shorty the story about how ol' Lefler caught a rattler for stew once. That ol' Lefler jes crawled up to a hole, waited for that sucker to poke its head out, and nabbed it slick as you please. Danged if I didn't see it with my own eyes. But Shorty gets suspicious of my stories now and then—"

"Suspicious! I flat out don't believe most of what comes out of his mouth!"

"—and he's sayin' that there one is a fib. Well sir, we spy a rattler hole up on the banks, past the cottonwoods, so I tell ol' Shorty I'm a-goin' to prove it can be done.

"So I ride up to that ol' hole and clamber down off my horse and sit there awhile, and all of a sudden there's this rattlin' in the grass above me. It's the rattler a-comin' home, and I know I'd better git, 'cause there ain't no chance to nab it now. I pull my pistol to shoot it, but I cain't see it, and it rattles again and my horse takes off into the river. Well, I take off after him, into the cold, and hit a sinkhole in the water and go under.

"I can't swim so good, and yell for Shorty. He rides up to pull me out and ends up in the water with me."

"He pulled me in," Shorty said. "Clean lost his head and pulled me off my horse."

"I never lost my head. You was jumpin' in to save me. I might have been a bit hasty," Jack conceded. "Anyway, we struggle to the bank—"

"We walked," Shorty said. "Wasn't no trouble to step out of that hole into shallow water, if Jack had kept his head."

"Shorty has a way of minimizing difficulty," Jack said. "But there we were in the cold, ridin' five miles wet to our underbritches, and well, here we are."

"And I'd surely hold it against Jack, except he looks a lot worse than me," Shorty said.

"Thing I regret most is not gettin' that rattler. Rattlesnake stew would sure taste mighty fine just about now." Jack sighed. "Mrs. Parsons makes the best chicken soup in the county, but a body can only down so much of it."

They both began to cough, so I ran down for their medicine and dosed them, then left them to sleep again. Despite all their teasing, they had the glittery eyes of men with fever, and I prayed all would go well with them.

6.
A Vision of Family Life
Tom

"Tom, go help Mr. Parsons with the horses," Mrs. Parsons said when I arrived in the kitchen, my arms loaded with dishes. I practically flew out the door, glad to escape the housework, but slowed down on approaching the barn. Mr. Parsons was not someone easy to be comfortable around.

Chester was easing the horses out of their stays. Chester was Evie's older brother, my age, taller and thinner than me. He had been sickly much of his childhood, and not around the country much, so I didn't know him as well as Evie. Far from sickly now, he moved and spoke with quick energy, much like his father.

He nodded to me. "Hello, Tom. Heard you were coming," he said. I led one of the sleek buggy horses to its stall, and he the other. Mr. Parsons and the two youngest children emerged from the tack room, where they'd been storing the buggy robes. "Hello, Tom," Mr. Parsons greeted me. His thick English accent always surprised me because he looked so American. "I suppose my wife's kept you busy?"

"Yes sir," I said.

"Found the bunkhouse?"

"Yes sir."

"Good, then. Chester and I will store the buggy, if you'll rub down the horses. These are Morgans, Dante and Faust, the horses for both the two- and the four-wheeled carriages. The Percherons there, Lady and Belle, pull the wagon and the plow, and the quarter horses handle the cattle. They're not broken for a carriage. I like to take care of all the buggy work myself, but you'll care for the live-stock, and the wagon if need be while you're here. Feed is in the granary there"—he pointed to a wooden bin built into the stable—"and brushes here." He handed me a brush and currycomb. "Store these in the tack room when you're done." He turned abruptly, nodded to Chester, and together they wheeled the buggy into its space, next to three other blanket-covered shapes, and, with the dubious aid of the children, Guy and Anna, covered it with a buffalo robe. With no more thought to me, Mr. Parsons strode to the house, the two little ones scampering behind him. Chester grinned at me apologetically. "I'd best go in as well," he said. "It's good you're here. See you at supper."

I groomed the Morgans carefully, marveling at their sleekness and strength, then led them to the water trough, stabled them, and brought buckets of grain to fill the feed troughs. Nine horses, including my own and Evie's, were under my care now. I did not have to muck out the stalls—not today, anyway. Someone had done that chore already. As I worked, I knocked on the walls of the huge barn and stomped on the thick wooden floor, searching for the other end of the tunnel Evie had mentioned, but finding nothing.

Chester appeared as I was finishing with the horses. "Mama said to call you to supper. Usually she rings a bell, but I told her I'd fetch you. Thought I'd help you with the stock, but you're already done. I like to work around them—it's the only ranch job I like—but there's not much chance. Papa would rather the hired men took care of them."

"I like being around them," I said. "Such fine animals, the Morgans."

Chester stroked the neck of the nearest horse. "They can both run like the devil. Papa has a weakness for buggies. We have the four-wheeler, and two two-wheeled buggies, one for Mama to use and one other."

"Do you drive them?"

"Sure—if Papa's not around. He's pretty picky. He lets me handle the cow ponies however I want, but Dante and Faust, well, he doesn't think I'm old enough. I can drive them fine though. Last summer, when Papa was gone, I drove them into town to court a gal, and they were something. Trouble was, Mama caught me. Now I'm not supposed to drive them at all. I don't get much chance anyway, being gone at school all week."

"Do your little brother and sister go to school?" I asked as we walked to the house.

"No. Guy's only six, and Anna five. There were two brothers between Guy and Evie, but they died before Guy was born. They were buried at our old home place, before Papa bought this one, but when we moved here, Papa and Mama had them buried in the new cemetery."

"Your papa didn't build this place?" The ranch looked so like Mr. Parsons, trying to be English yet only succeeding in being something uniquely suited to this land.

"No, another Englishman built it. But before he'd lived here very long his wife died, drowned in the horse trough, and he couldn't stand to stay here with the memory."

I'd never heard this story before. "Murder, suicide, or accident?"

He shook his head. "They called it an accident. But nobody could say for sure."

I glanced back at the horse trough and shivered. The story cast the trough in a new and sinister light altogether. I'd think differently about being around the barn in the dark after this.

We'd reached the back door. "Where can I wash up?" I asked, realizing I must smell like a combination of sickroom and stable.

The house had a small washroom off the back porch. I couldn't enter the main house from it, so I had to go to the porch again and then in the back door, through the kitchen, and into the dining room, where everyone was gathered around the table.

"Wheat's the coming crop, Hildy," Mr. Parsons remarked to his wife. "They're saying in the *Stockman's Quarterly*, no more planting the yeoman's four." At her puzzled expression, he explained: "That is magazine talk for wheat, corn, oats, and barley, in equal measure. Every farmer around here plants now as they did in the East, but we're figuring out this country's best for wheat crops, if we can settle on what kind of wheat, and soon we'll plant nothing but."

Mrs. Parsons listened as attentively as she could while carrying heaping dishes to the table, admonishing the little ones to sit still, and filling all the glasses with icy water from an indoor pump at the sink. She asked after different families in town, and he answered in monosyllables. Finally, apron still on, Mrs. Parsons sank into the chair opposite Mr. Parsons at the end of the oak table, sighed, and said, "Shall we say grace?"

Their heads bowed at once, and I ducked mine as well, listening to Mr. Parsons give a lengthy account of things his children should be grateful were provided for them, with the Lord's help. He ended with a request for the welfare of the sick cowboys, said a quick amen, and began passing the bowls of food. The bowls went every which way, quickly, with Mr. Parsons directing, so that no one took a bite before every plate was filled, and every plate was filled to bursting in an amazingly short time. Then everyone fell to eating as if half starved, Mrs. Parsons pointing out breaches in table etiquette and Mr. Parsons picking up his one-sided discussion of wheat farming as if he'd never left off.

"I read that they're even experimenting with irrigation techniques," he said, "to prove that the ingenuity of man can best the caprices of nature. Grain will grow where it's never been possible before, and turn this dry prairie into a man-made paradise. I might try something myself, with that field over by the Chikaskia. But some country is best left to cattle—what? There's fortune enough to be made in beef, and not so much risk with the weather.

"Well, Thomas," he said abruptly, turning to me, "what do you make of our place here? Spacious, don't you think? Built to be an exact replica of an English manor house. Sixteen rooms, every scrap imported from England, even the doorknobs. Cedar planks for the siding, two thicknesses of oak and cherry flooring. We've made changes as need be—the front porch, for example, is adapted from the American Southwest. Adobe. It stays cooler during the droughts. And the barn, adapted to accommodate a number of animals and buggies. Larger than you'll find in the typical English countryside, more like a New England barn. Still, the spirit of the Old World is remarkably preserved, even down to the wine cellar in the basement."

"It's quite a fine place," I offered, unsure whether he wanted an answer or not.

"None like it in the area. You may have heard of that Scotsman who's building a castle on the banks of the Arkansas River, near Wichita. Limestone walls, turreted tower, everything but a moat, and the river will provide that. Sheer vanity. This isn't a feudal system we're creating out here, after all."

"Yes sir."

"Wonderful supper, my dear," he said to Mrs. Parsons, pushing back his chair. In this respect, at least, their family was like mine. The entire meal, which took Mrs. Parsons all afternoon to fix, was inhaled in less than fifteen minutes.

The promised popcorn appeared in the parlor after the young ones had their bath in a copper tub behind a screen in the kitchen and were sent to bed. The evening was quiet, though lively compared to my father's place. Evie and Chester took turns reading out loud from a magazine story, while Mr. Parsons looked over his mail, Mrs. Parsons knitted, and I polished my boots, at Mrs. Parsons's suggestion. No one quarreled, no one was too exhausted to participate, no one was hungry, ill-clad, or cold. Lamplight gleamed at the end of the kitchen table where they read, and firelight from the cookstove cast red shadows on the other. It struck me that this vision of family life might be worth having, regardless of what Mr. Parsons had had to do to get it.

Too soon I had to head for the bunkhouse. I didn't believe in ghosts, but the horse trough looked forlorn and cut off. The globe of light from my lantern cast shadows, made the darkness around me darker.

I fumbled to get the bunkhouse door open. The lantern brightened the room as I built a fire in the stove, and the room quickly warmed. I dimmed the lantern to save oil and sat thinking by the stove's light.

Evie was what I thought about. I wished she didn't have to go away the next day. I kept seeing how she looked in the lamplight, kept hearing her whisper, "I will, soon enough," when I'd asked her to show me the tunnel to the barn. She had caught my eye a few times at supper and after, but hadn't spoken, and that made me irritated and wanting to be with her all the more. Was I just a new face to break the monotony? Someone who didn't count because he was hired help? Being around her made me feel like I did when I tried to catch silver-flecked minnows in the creek, standing knee-deep in clear water as they darted just through my fingers, spinning around after them till my head swam.

7.
Girlish Desires
Evie

After Tom left, I excused myself and holed up in my room, brushed my hair, and wished I didn't have to go back to town the next day. From the window in the parlor, I'd seen him ride up the lane in the morning, and I'd waited. From the window in my room now, the glow of his lantern in the bunkhouse was visible.

I hated feeling the way I did about Tom Hunter, but I didn't know what to do about it. Ever since I'd met him, with his dark hair and eyes, his gentlemanly ways and soft voice, I'd felt the way you feel at a beautiful sunset, when the sky streaks rose and gold. Such a longing rises up in you. Yet anger rises too, because the sun sets over the same ordinary land it always has. It's just fooling you temporarily.

So maybe it was good I was leaving tomorrow. He'd be there at home when I came back, and at school I wouldn't have to think about him.

I was no fool. I knew I couldn't marry him. At sixteen, a girl was supposed to consider these things about the boys she met. I was, at Mama's direction, embroidering pillowcases and keeping my eyes open should somebody eligible look my way. *Eligible* meant someone with property and standing—Tom didn't even come close. What Mama didn't realize was that I didn't care about looking for someone suitable. Papa said I always wanted what I couldn't have, and in more ways than one he was right. He'd never let me have the ranch.

Sitting at the window brushing my hair, I stared past my father's outbuildings to what I couldn't see in the darkness but knew was there. My bedroom window looked out to the southwest, over grassy swells that sloped to the wooded line of the Chikaskia River about five miles distant. Papa owned all that land and claimed grazing rights to five times that area. Somewhere, five cattle, bought by me with money I had earned, wandered the length and breadth of that country without any restrictions. One day Chester would inherit the land, because he was the oldest boy. And I wanted it.

I stood up, bent over at the waist, and brushed my hair upside down. A hundred strokes every night. This was an order of Mama's I didn't rebel against, because the prairie sun was drying. I intended to be out in it as much as I could, so I protected my hair. Maybe I was vain about it. It swept the backs of my knees when I stood up. I looked at myself in the mirror a good long time, even with Mama's cautions against vanity running through my mind. I saw the reflection of my cut-glass lotion bottle and the silver back of my brush as they lay on the oak dressing table. And then me. Amid the flowered walls of my bedroom I stood framed by the oak window casing, behind which, in the dark, rolled the wild prairie grass.

8.

Book Talk

Evie

High school dragged by same as ever, endless. Much as I liked my girlfriends, I couldn't stand the cooped-up feeling of brick walls and the educational smell of waxed floors. Town was confining too. I might walk to the store with Hazel in nice weather, but in cold and rain all I could do was sit inside and study. The relief was that I could read. *The Adventures of Huckleberry Finn* took me out of the wet and sent me rolling downriver in the warm South.

The next weekend that I was home, I ran into Tom on my way upstairs. He was carrying a tray from the sick men's room. He smiled. I just mumbled a greeting and retreated to my room, but later I went looking for him. I found him in the barn.

"So what did you think?" I asked him.

"About what?"

"About my reading material, *Huckleberry Finn.* Did you finish it?" I hopped up on the granary lid and made myself comfortable, watching him work.

"I did. Not much else to do lately, evenings. Did you?"

"Almost. What was your favorite part?"

He stopped brushing Lady, one of my father's Percherons, to consider. "I just like the idea of Huck breaking away to be free."

"Me too," I said. "And how clever he was. Dressing up like a girl to get news about himself, for one thing."

"Pretty clever the way he got found out, too, threading a needle and catching a lump of lead like a boy."

"Only I'm surprised the woman even got suspicious of him. Most people don't look past appearance."

Tom looked at me carefully for a moment, then began brushing again. I squirmed, a little uncomfortable. Did he think I didn't look past appearances?

He said, "That's the point. Maybe not of that scene, but of the book. Most of those characters just act out of beliefs they don't even think about, like the Hatfields and McCoys. Or take Jim, the slave. Most people never thought of him having a family and wanting to be free like anybody else."

I watched Tom's face as he spoke. He'd stopped looking at me, didn't look at anything, as if he was looking at what he said as he said it. I was seeing into the heart of him, like I had before, in our basement. And as before, it made me feel slightly out of breath. I noticed too what a fine mouth he had, firm but soft.

I said, "Well, sure, colored folks would want to be free, same as anybody. That's what the war was about, after all. The folks in Kansas were the first to fight for that."

"That's not the way they told it back in Virginia. Although back in Virginia, nobody ever talked about slave times. My grandparents' colored help must have once been their slaves—" He stopped talking for a moment, then looked at me. "Imagine my grandparents owning people! But they never said a word."

"Maybe they were ashamed, or didn't like to think about it. People don't like change, even if it's for the better." Maybe I could remind him I wasn't like my folks, just as he wasn't like his grandparents. "Take my friends and me. We talk about getting to vote. But our parents don't want to hear it. They're just more stuck in their ways than we are. Now, that's not the same as ending slavery, but still."

"You aren't going to start marching and carrying signs, are you?"

"The town ladies, some of them do. The newspaper editor writes ridiculous things about them. He says next thing they'll be wanting to cut their hair and wear pants."

Tom laughed. "Sounds like he's worried they might get their way."

"Still, that doesn't make them men. And mercy on us if a woman gets her way!"

"Aw now, I wouldn't imagine you have much trouble."

There was a sudden silence between us. It felt good, next to him. His eyes had the finest flecks of light. I started to lean closer, but caught myself. He looked down at my hand as if to take it.

"I'd better go," I said.

He didn't call out after me as I walked out of the barn. That vexed me a bit.

9.

A Christmas Eve Tale

Tom

Cold winter rains and winds kept Evie and Chester in town for the next several weekends. I was just as glad not to have to think about Evie Parsons, although I did anyway, some. The cold also kept Shorty and Jack in their room recovering, so I continued double duty as hired hand and nursemaid. The morning before Christmas, Mrs. Parsons asked me to go chop down a cedar tree in the pasture and drag it home. "Get one with a pretty shape, not too tall, one that'll make a good Christmas tree."

"A cedar tree?"

"To decorate for Christmas."

"Yes ma'am, but those are scrubby little things, not proper Christmas trees."

"As proper as can be, you'll see. We put it up in the house and hang pretty paper decorations on it, and string popcorn strands on it, and it looks grand. You ought to put lighted candles in it, but Mr. Parsons believes there's a risk of fire, so we leave those off. He could do without the tree altogether—he's from England, you know—but he must have the children get their gifts on Christmas Eve!"

I'd almost forgotten that a body could celebrate at Christmas. Papa and Mattie had let us have as fine a dinner as Mattie could scrounge up, and a gift of clothing for each of us children, sent from my grandparents and opened under scowls from Papa and Mattie, who resented charity. That was all there had been to those Christmases. Never a tree. Caleb and Emma had only those toys they could invent for themselves, and no niceties at all. A dress or pair of socks came as soon as the old ones wore out, if we could afford it, and if not we made do.

Of course in Virginia, my grandparents had spoiled me. There would be a grand fir, the kind that didn't grow out on the plains, and a heap of sausages on Christmas morning, and candy at my plate, and gifts of toys, and always a feast for dinner, shared with neighbors and folks from town, and often dancing after.

"Do you want to go home tomorrow, Tom, spend Christmas with your folks?" Mrs. Parsons asked as we stood the tree in the parlor by one of the staircases. I'd nailed two boards crosswise to the tree bottom so that it would stand upright.

"If you don't mind, ma'am, I'll just spend the day in the bunkhouse." I doubted they'd welcome me at home.

"Heavens, if that's what you want, but we'd be glad for you to join us. This afternoon we'll decorate the tree and give the little ones their gifts, and then make the drive to town for church. And tomorrow I'll have a dinner for you and Shorty and Jack in the kitchen, and you can come to the dance tomorrow night. This country's lonely enough as it is without anyone needing to be alone on Christmas."

And so I spent Christmas as part of the Parsons family, yet not part of it as well.

Evie came home. I spotted her getting out of the buggy. She glanced at me, smiled, and looked away.

That afternoon in the parlor, Mr. Parsons had a huge log blazing in the fireplace, which took up the whole space between the double staircase. Everyone, dressed in all their finery, gathered around, sitting carefully on the sofas and settees. Shorty and Jack felt well enough to come down for the festivities, and didn't cough on anyone. Mrs. Parsons brought out trays of tea cakes, some of a kind I'd never tasted before, a strong anise-flavored shortbread from her old-world family recipes. We munched and sipped tea and strung popcorn on thread with needles. Lightning Jack told cowboy tall tales as I helped the children drape the popcorn strings around the tree and fasten colored paper pictures, stars, mangers, angels, and Holy Families to the branches. Once, I got close enough to Evie to accidentally brush her hand as we reached for the same branch, but she just moved away and didn't so much as look at me. I had no gift for her and had worried about it, but I was glad now. How would I get through the evening at church, being with Evie yet not able to be with her? I'd not even spoken to her yet and didn't see any likelihood of it.

After the tree was fixed up, the children sat cross-legged in front of the fireplace, even Chester and Evie, and Mr. Parsons doled out gifts from a basket behind the sofa. These were all toys or frivolities. Evie got a fine set of combs, and I let myself imagine how they'd gleam against her hair.

"Play for us, Shorty, if you feel up to it," Mrs. Parsons said, and Shorty obliged, drawing out the fiddle he'd brought from the bunkhouse.

"When I was smaller than Anna there, in slave times, my old master give me a fiddle and made me play it for his parties. It's the only thing I took with me when freedom come," Shorty said as he rosined the bow. "Mighty comforting on a lonely plain."

"Well, we won't expect you to play for us tomorrow night, but you're welcome to come sit, if you feel well enough. You too, Jack, and Tom," Mrs. Parsons said.

"Thank you, ma'am."

The fiddle's voice rasped and wailed, and then notes sounded, drawn out and true, and Shorty's voice joined them.

Foller, foller, rise up, shepherd, an' foller
Foller the star of Bethlehem
Rise up, shepherd, an' foller.
If you take good heed to the angel's words

Rise up, shepherd, an' foller
You'll forget yo' flocks, you'll forget yo' herds
Rise up, shepherd, an' foller.

The melody washed over us in a plaintive protest. Then the fiddle went silent, and Shorty declared himself tired out.

"Your turn, Tom. What can you do?" Mrs. Parsons asked. Startled, I looked at her blankly. My sense of being part of the family evaporated and I felt like the hired hand again, hired to entertain. I struggled to think of something. A poem from my lonely herding days spent reading on the prairie came back to me.

"I can recite a poem," I said.

Mr. Parsons looked surprised, and Mrs. Parsons said, "One that's fit for young ears, I trust."

"Yes ma'am." Who did she think I was, anyway?

I stood up. "It's a long poem by Keats. I just remember part of it. The lord of the house throws a big party, and his daughter has heard the legend that if a girl goes to bed at midnight without supper and falls asleep without thinking of anything but heaven, she'll dream of her future husband." I cleared my throat, cleared it again, and began:

They told her how, upon St. Agnes' Eve,
Young virgins might have visions of delight,
And soft adorings from their loves receive
Upon the honey'd middle of the night . . .

I worked up the courage to look at Evie as I spoke, but couldn't read the expression on her face. I kept on, hoping she knew this was for her.

Full of this whim was thoughtful Madeline:
The music, yearning like a god in pain,
She scarcely heard: her maiden eyes divine,
Fix'd on the floor, saw many a sweeping train
Pass by—she heeded not at all: in vain
Came many a tiptoe, amorous cavalier,
And back retir'd, not cool'd by high disdain,
But she saw not: her heart was otherwhere:
She sigh'd for Agnes' dreams, the sweetest of the year.

I left out the part about how Madeline's lover, despised by her family because of his own family, sneaks into her bedroom and convinces her to run off with him.

Mrs. Parsons frowned, first at me and then at her daughter. But all she said was, "Thank you, young man."

It only got worse later, when Mrs. Parsons gave me an old suit of Chester's to wear. The suit fit fine, but that wasn't the point. The family drove the buggy to church, and I followed behind on my horse. They put me at the far end of the pew. And after services, Evie got swallowed up by a group of girls from her school. I stood at the bottom of the church steps, not recognizing anyone but the storekeeper, who only nodded to me.

Then two boys passed whom I knew from herding cows in the summer. I started to go to them, but heard them talking about algebra at school, and suddenly all the pride I'd built up at working a ranch drained away. The world that contained algebra, and high school, was a world I was forever cut off from by necessity and by choice, a choice I'd never regretted until that moment. I backed away.

I felt no shame at being a farmer's son. A farmer worked for no one but himself, and the flat prairie gave the illusion of equality. Yet even though I'd lived here four years, somewhere inside I'd always thought of myself as the Virginia judge's grandson. Though I'd hated it, there was privilege attached. Maybe the borrowed clothes made it worse, but Christmas Eve, standing there at the bottom of the church steps, I realized I had no more privilege. The deaths of my grandparents ended that. Everything depended on what I could do for someone else, and what they in turn would do for me.

No wonder Mrs. Parsons wanted to keep me away from Evie.

10.
Homecoming
Evie

The week away from school took its time coming, but finally arrived. While at Miss Watkins's, I truly minded not being home getting ready for Christmas. I liked to help Mama bake her fancy yeast breads, and tea cakes with anise, and pies— the sour cream and raisin with sweet meringue on top was my favorite. I loved pinching dough to snack on, loved the warmth and fragrance of the kitchen, and Mama and little Anna and me laughing. At Miss Watkins's I passed the time before break making gifts, embroidered handkerchiefs for Papa and my brothers, a doll dress for Anna, a roll of crocheted lace for Mama.

But what a relief to step down from the buggy! I had been too long away this time, what with the nasty weather. I hugged Mama and the little ones tight, told Mama the news from town, chattering all the way inside. As soon as possible though, after I was settled in and had grabbed one of the tea cakes, I raced upstairs, put on my riding clothes, and headed for the barn, where Andromeda greeted me with a whicker.

My pony loved the tea cake, and I was surely glad to see her. I brushed her, admiring again the *V*-shaped constellation of white spots on her brown back. She didn't mind a bit when I put the saddle and bridle on, even though it had been close to a month since I'd ridden her. We took out across the pasture, and out of sight of the house I let her go as fast as she would, galloping free.

I rode down to the Chikaskia, crossed at the shallow ford, and headed downriver to Clearwater Creek. This was where I often found my cattle, all five of them, on their winter range. I scouted the pastureland and found four, all with swollen bellies. They looked to be in fine shape for delivering their calves in spring. The fifth cow was nowhere around, but there were no signs of trouble. She was bound to be somewhere, and it was time to get back.

Just past the creek, I turned around and galloped to the barn. A distance away I pulled up short, for I'd seen Tom carrying wood to the house. I fought down my pleasure, realizing I'd been hoping he'd spend Christmas with us. He was clear away from the barn before I took my pony in, rubbed her down, and gave her a pail of oats.

He and the other cowboys joined us for Christmas Eve. The other hands dressed up, but Tom didn't, and I guessed maybe he didn't have anything nice. He was clean and combed, though, and my but he was handsome. A gentleman still, even in his rough clothes.

My mother caught my admiring glance and frowned. She had a sixth sense when it came to boys around me. I couldn't look, couldn't even breathe differently around certain boys. Other boys, such as the ones who would come for dinner tomorrow, I couldn't pay enough attention to. Part of my grooming, for the suitable marriage partner. I wished she'd just let me be.

I ignored him as best I could, so she wouldn't worry. My breath caught, though, when his hand accidentally brushed mine as we decorated the tree. I didn't know a boy's touch could make the ground feel unsteady.

After we decorated the tree we gave each other gifts we'd chosen. It was small stuff, handkerchiefs from Chester, drawings from Guy, embroidery from Anna, combs from my parents, but I loved the intimacy of the gift-giving. Then the cowboys performed for us, and even in front of my family, it was pretty hard to ignore Tom when he recited poetry. I'd never heard anything more beautiful, and never thought words like that could come from him. He'd quit school after eighth grade.

His words moved more than me. After he left to do chores, Mama said, "That Tom's a well-spoken young man."

"We did the right thing, getting him out of that home," Papa said. "He would have starved in more ways than one if he'd had to stay there."

"I don't think he has a suit to wear, did you notice?"

"Mama, maybe you could give him one of Chester's," I said.

"Yes, that might do, but I don't want to embarrass him, Evie. I don't want him thinking he's a charity case."

"He won't think that. He'll look nice."

Church was another thing about Christmas I really liked, what with the carols and the Bible stories and all. I liked church anyway. It was hot in summer and cold in winter, but the Reverend Hankins spoke his heart. The Christmas Eve sermon was about how the Christ Child fooled everyone by being born in a stable. The good reverend followed the theme he preached on most often: folks have to look behind what they see on the outside. I liked that because I hated to have people look at me and see only what they wanted to see (as did most folks around here, including certain parents).

I was glad Jack and Shorty stayed home, frankly, because Jack was pretty crude and wicked for a church, what with his drinking and gambling, and Shorty, well, colored people didn't come to our church. I didn't know where they went. But I was glad Tom came with us. He must have appreciated the sermon too, after what he'd said about *Huckleberry Finn*. He looked very handsome in Chester's suit, and I was pleased to have thought of it. He'd been quiet, even more than usual, and at church he puzzled me when he acted stiff and standoffish. He stood around frowning by himself after the service, like he didn't want anyone near him, so I kept away, even though the crowd allowed us the opportunity to talk together. I started toward him once, to find out what was wrong, but he flushed and walked away angrily—not angry with me, he couldn't have seen me—but something had his dander up.

II.
Christmas Day
Tom

Christmas morning was like any other morning. I got up, broke ice in the trough to water the stock, milked the cows, swept out the barn, gathered the eggs, and washed up for breakfast. Jack and Shorty, even though the pneumonia had cleared, still took meals in their sickroom, partly because they slept late in the mornings, partly because Mrs. Parsons still didn't want them around the family much. So I sat down with the family Christmas morning. There were fried eggs and pork sausages and pancakes and more of the anise shortbreads, which Mrs. Parsons dipped in her coffee. And beside every plate was a little round cake and a small pile of horehound candy.

Mrs. Parsons was as friendly to me as ever, but she set my plate at the far end of the table from Evie's.

I was usually quiet, and Guy and Anna's chatter more than made up for any lapses on my part, so my silence wasn't noticed.

After breakfast Mr. Parsons and Chester moved the buggies and wagon out of the barn, while I swept the wide main floor and carried a table from the house to the far wall, to set food on for the dance that evening. We lay down a wooden hay platform, about five feet by five feet, for the fiddlers to stand on, and generally made the barn look presentable. Then Mr. Parsons told Chester and me to go get ourselves cleaned up, as it was about time for the guests to arrive. In the bunkhouse I brushed the dust off the borrowed suit; washed my face, hands, and teeth; shaved; combed my hair; recombed it; and wished I had more to work with in the way of making myself look good.

They came in buggies, two ranching families and the banker's brood. I helped the ladies descend and led the carriages behind the barn, stabled the horses, and stacked whatever hampers of food they'd brought for the dance, piling it all on the table in the barn and shooing the barn cats away.

Then it was Christmas dinner at the kitchen table with Jack and Shorty, and I tried to make cracks about their being too weak to work but strong enough to eat. Yet my mind was on the dining room, where everyone else ate with the guests. I wondered whom Evie sat beside. Two or three young men had been among the company that alighted from the buggies.

At my grandparents' Christmas dinners, Grandfather's smoked ham was slathered with Grandmother's own curried cranberry sauce, the buttermilk pie fairly drowned in its own richness, and the room shimmered with the glint of candlelight on china and crystal, glowed with warmth, only partly from the eggnog Grandfather brought out to end the Christmas meal. I wondered what my sister, Becky, was doing on this first Christmas without the old ones.

"Tom?" Shorty said. "Where'd you drift off to?"

"I was just thinking of Christmas in Virginia," I said.

"You still have family there?"

"Just my sister." I didn't say any more, so they changed the subject. I hadn't told Shorty or Jack anything about my grandparents, or about their deaths.

After dinner, Jack and Shorty and I did dishes, so Mrs. Parsons wouldn't have to, although she might as well have, the way she fussed around us. She did not surrender her kitchen easily.

When more folks began arriving for the dance, I led them not to the main house but directly to the barn, where the women piled more food on the table. About thirty people had gathered by the time the fiddlers warmed up. My father and step-family were not among them, and neither were any of the German immigrants. In fact, no one looked familiar.

Evie came to the barn then, in her velvet-trimmed Christmas frock, which made her look taller and even more grown up. She wore her hair up, held by her new combs, and she was so grand I was afraid to look at her, yet couldn't help myself. She was still with her friends, and I kept my distance.

Shorty and Jack claimed to be too tired for the dance, but they came down to talk to the other ranch hands, who lounged around the edges of the dancing. The cowboys kept mostly to themselves, except when one of the ranch wives would urge more food on them, and now and then one of the white hands would dance with a girl. Once in a while they'd fill in a square as needed, some of them even dancing the woman's part, since there were more men than women.

I stood with the loungers and heard their talk of cattle roping and branding. Uncomfortable at asking to be part of the dancing group, I stood with the ones that didn't dance, watching Evie bow to her partner, bow to her corner, and take off in a velvet swirl as the fiddle wailed.

The talk turned to what was in front of us. Every man of us, ranchers, ranchers' sons, and ranch hands alike, had been taught to be respectful to ladies, and these were all ladies dancing. Yet when the ladies weren't within hearing distance, some of the men didn't feel so constrained by upbringing. Not just the ranch hands, either. The ranchers and sons, including Chester, stood with us at times and joined in. Some said things the ladies wouldn't have cared to hear said about themselves. The unspoken rule was that no one said anything about your wife, sister, sweetheart, or mother. When Chester left, the talk turned to Evie, and I told them to stop. "Boy, she'll never be your sweetheart, what's the matter with you?"

they said, and I walked away, the blood pounding in my ears. I stumbled blindly to the table and helped myself to the food, then one of the older women pulled me into a square, and I danced on until, by some miracle, I found myself partnered with Evie for the reel.

12.
A Cardinal Rule
Evie

Christmas morning Anna woke me up by jumping on my bed. "Get up, Evie, won't you?"

We woke the family and hurried to dress. Then, off to help Mama with breakfast. I was pleased to see that Tom joined us, but again was forced to keep my distance.

Then there was Christmas dinner to get through. Mama's dinners were always wonderful, and this year she had ham and a wild turkey Papa had shot the day before, and her good yeast breads, and pickles, beets, potatoes, and onions, and Christmas cake and plum pudding, Papa's favorite, for dessert. But I had to sit by Riley Kendricks, who was five years older than me and designated "suitable," and all he talked about was the Christmas hunt. (He and Mr. Kendricks had gone hunting with Papa the day before.) Now, Papa had taught me how to shoot, in case of rattlers or rabid animals, and Papa and Mama both hunted (Mama liked to shoot rabbits from the buggy—protecting her garden, she said), but I had no love for killing wild things. I liked to see them run free. So Riley's talk was unendurable and more than a little boastful, especially since he'd shot only one turkey. I was an admirable hostess for listening to him go on, but couldn't help telling him it was cruel to kill for sport.

"It's not just sport. We eat everything we kill," he said.

"But you like it too much," I replied.

Our conversation died right there, and I spent the rest of dinner listening to Matthew Hornby, age eleven and seated to my other side, discuss catching salamanders in the creek come spring, which, to be honest, was more interesting. Matthew swore to me he always let them go. What a gentleman.

Finally it was time for the dance, where an unexpected situation didn't take long to present itself.

Mama always grumbled about a Christm̄ dance, what with her Methodist upbringing, which didn't approve of dancing. "And on Christmas too!" she'd say. But this was one of Papa's English traditions that he wouldn't let go. "It's civilized dancing, after all, even if it is in a barn. A proper celebration," he'd argue. So Mama would relent every year, but she kept an eye out for anything improper.

When I took a break from the dancing, about an hour after the start, I stood with the girls in the corner of the barn and compared the men: who was handsomest, strongest, whom they'd most like to be carried away to the bunkhouse by. My mother might have been shocked to hear how frank the talk became, but these girls grew up around barnyards and weren't shy about the workings of nature. The talk of that kind, though, wasn't about anyone who was someone's brother or father—too boring or old or closely related. So that left the cowboys, who were kind of mysterious anyway. The girls were proper enough not to talk that way about anyone of a different race, and silly enough to ignore the old and the ugly, so that left the ones like Tom open for discussion, and Tom got his share. But I couldn't laugh at what they said; I told them to hush up, which was as good as announcing that I was sweet on him.

Disgusted with them, and with myself, I turned away and rejoined the dance, and as the set ended came face to face with Tom as my partner for the reel.

Reeling doesn't leave time for talking. You gallop up and down in front of everyone, holding each other so close your head spins, then you both dissolve in laughter at the end. I was a pretty frank talker, and I'd kissed a boy or two in town, but I lacked experience with ones I might really like, so the feeling of him holding me close, even just for a dance, was . . . let me say I felt so good it hurt to breathe.

At the end of the reel, my mother bore down on Tom and me and steered me away from him into a group of her friends, where I was systematically distracted for the next half hour answering questions about how Miss Watkins helped me make (forced me to make) my Christmas dress. As soon as possible, I escaped. I didn't want to rejoin my friends, and found I'd lost interest in dancing since Tom was no longer among those on the dance floor. Ducking out the barn door, I made my way among the men outside smoking and headed for the house, glad to be out in the cold air.

By the water trough, I saw a figure and thought it was the ghost. When we first moved onto the place, Chester and I had scared ourselves with ghost sightings of the woman who'd been found dead in the trough, and once I really had seen a shadowy being leaning over it. It had been years since the trough had frightened me, but my heart pounded just the same. The pounding only increased when I realized the figure was Tom.

He stood as he saw me approach.

"I didn't follow you," I said. "The air just got thick in there with my mother's friends breathing down my neck."

"You give them something to talk about?"

"If you call how I made my Christmas dress something to talk about." I mimicked the women inside: "My, what a nice job you did with the bodice interfacing!"

He eyed me in a way I hadn't seen before, and said, "That bodice is something to talk about in my book."

This was a boldness I hadn't expected in him. But it didn't make me draw back. "It's surely more interesting to hear you talk about it," I replied.

I leaned close and kissed him then.

"I've been wanting to do that for so long," he said.

"Why hadn't you then?" I breathed.

"You haven't wanted me anywhere near you since you got home."

"What if I did? There's eyes and ears everywhere, even so."

"Not in the bunkhouse."

"Criminy, what do you think I am?" I whispered, pushing away.

"No, Evie, I meant to talk. No eyes and ears there. That's all. Please." He looked sincere.

A cardinal rule for girls growing up on ranches: Never go into the bunkhouse. Mama had drilled that into me from the time I could remember. Ranch girls might talk about cowboys, but they tended to weigh their options too carefully to follow through.

I went with him to see if I could trust him.

13.

A Young Lady in the Cowboys' Bunkhouse

Tom

I think when she followed me to the bunkhouse she was testing me, to see if I meant what I said. She sat on the bunk bed more carefully than I'd ever seen her move. I sat on the opposite bunk.

"So," she said.

"So," I said.

She looked around the room curiously. "I haven't been in here since I was a little girl."

"Why not?"

She stared at me. "Young ladies don't go into cowboys' bunkhouses."

"I didn't mean—I mean, I didn't think you

would, I just meant, since you lived here . . . Well, what do you think of the place?"

"Fine. It's fine."

I couldn't think of what to say.

"You look very pretty in that dress," I ventured at last.

"We've already discussed my dress."

Another pause.

"You look handsome in that suit," she offered.

"Thank you. It was nice of your mother to lend it to me."

"Oh, you can keep it. Chester's done with it. It was my idea to give it to you."

"Your idea?"

She studied my face. "Oh no. It made you feel bad, didn't it? Like taking charity."

"No." If it was a gift from Evie, it wasn't so bad. Anyway, I couldn't have her feeling sorry for me.

"Liar."

We sat awhile longer without speaking.

"So, what did you want to talk about?" she asked finally.

I'd been trying to think of all the things I'd wanted to say to her since she'd been home, but they all evaporated with her nearness. I folded and refolded my hands, shifted my weight on the bunk.

Suddenly voices were right outside the window, a man's and a woman's, clear as day. "Shame on you," the woman said. "Does your mama know you talk like that?"

"Mama's down in Texas, sayin' her prayers for her wayward son," the man's voice replied. They both laughed, and their laughter grew fainter as they walked away.

Evie stood up. "I'd better go."

"Why?"

"We're going to get caught if I stay, that's why."

"No, listen. Those folks weren't paying attention to anyone but themselves."

"Look, you didn't want to talk after all."

"I do. How's school?"

"Fine." She looked out the window. "Criminy, more folks are coming."

"They won't see us, unless they see you leaving." She sat back down on the opposite bunk.

"Did you finish *Huckleberry Finn?*" I asked.

"Yes. I'm not surprised Huck didn't go back home, after running away. Sometimes home gets awful confining."

"Evie, you know, you have it pretty good here."

"It must sound loco to you, hearing me complain about a home with good parents who give me everything. It's just . . . when I was small, I rode all over these plains. I thought I could do anything. Then suddenly, I'm grown up and they change the rules."

"They just want what's best for you." Even as I said that, I saw in my mind the receipt in the ledger book, *To Thomas Hunter in receipt of check.* What my parents had thought was best would have killed my soul if I hadn't left.

"Best for me." She sighed. "Did you know Chester doesn't even want this ranch? He wants to marry a girl in town and be a storekeeper. We both want the opposite of what our parents want for us. They should have switched us."

"I don't understand Chester. If somebody was offering me a ranch, I would surely take it."

She looked at me funny. "You know, you won't gain anything by being with me."

"What?"

"If you hope to gain for yourself by pursuing me, it won't work."

Maybe, in some tiny but evil part of my mind, the thought of acquiring the ranch through her had occurred, and maybe that's why I got offended. "See here, you give me cast-off clothes because you feel sorry for me, then you kiss me, then you think I just want you for your ranch! It seems you have a very mixed opinion of me, Miss Parsons."

"Well, what am I supposed to think? You drag me into the bunkhouse, knowing the risk for us both, then you say you want the ranch."

"That's not what . . . I didn't . . . Look here, I'm not like you think."

"No? Well, I'm not like you think either." Good and mad now, she stood up and flounced out, not even bothering to be sure no people were around to see her leave.

Oh, what a mess. It probably started when I made that comment about her bodice. A gentleman shouldn't make remarks like that.

14.
From the Frying Pan Into the Fire
Evie

I didn't mean to just leave him sitting there mad. I hated the way the whole escapade went. But it was one thing to sneak away from Miss Watkins, another to break my parents' most solemn rule right under their noses at Christmas!

He must have thought I was pretty forward to kiss him. I shouldn't have done that. Maybe that's why he thought he could take me to the bunkhouse. Only he had been a gentleman there, until he made that crack about taking the ranch if offered. I didn't believe he was with me just to get the ranch. But then again, there were families who were interested in the land that would make my dowry. Riley Kendricks's family, for example. It was a sensitive point.

And I'd shamed Tom with the suit.

So I walked out.

He didn't look at me the next day, when he came to the house to help Shorty and Jack move their things back to the bunkhouse, but his ears got red. At supper he ignored me.

The next morning, after breakfast, I murmured to Mama something about needing to exercise my pony. She just said, "Don't be too long about it, you have sewing to do." I bolted outside to the barn, hoping to find Tom alone, but all the hired men were gathered, oiling harnesses. Tom barely mumbled a greeting, although Shorty and Jack were glad to talk to me.

"Tom here's so relieved to not have to play nursemaid anymore, he can hardly speak," Lightning Jack said.

"Now that we're up and around some we can start to undo all the damage he done around here," Shorty teased.

A horrible thought took hold of me then: now that Shorty and Jack were better, Tom might go home. We'd never speak to each other again as friends.

"Naw, it'd take too long. Besides, we may want him around for roundup," Jack said.

I hoped the relief didn't show in my face as it flooded through the rest of me. Papa always hired extra men, and Tom was bound to be one of them. The roundup wouldn't start until March, which meant Tom would likely stay on here until then.

But I'd still never get to talk to Tom alone, if the others were going to be hanging around.

I was glad for the chance to ride. The day was bright and cold, and the rhythm of Andromeda's trot cleared my head. I loved riding down the gentle sweep of the swell that ended by the river. Five fat cows with my brand greeted me there. This part of my life, anyway, was moving along fine. I'd have ten cattle in the spring and be able to start selling them in a year.

When I brought my pony in, Tom was by himself in the barn, sweeping out. I dismounted, and before even seeing to Andromeda, I took my chance. "About after the dance . . . ," I began.

He stopped me. "I shouldn't have taken you in there. Forget it."

"I don't think you're after the ranch."

"I could tell, from the way you took off."

"You don't understand. Some boys, or their parents, want the land. I'm . . . likely to end up marrying one of those boys."

We were both silent then, not looking at each other.

"I'm ashamed about that suit . . . ," I said.

He turned to face me then, surprised. "You're ashamed?"

I nodded. "I don't look down on you, Tom. I just thought how nice you'd look in it." I hardly ever blush, but it was my turn then.

He looked down at the floor. "It doesn't matter about the suit." He turned away and started sweeping again. I unsaddled Andromeda, took the bridle off, rubbed her down, and gave her oats. When I looked around, Tom had gone.

Later, in my room, I wondered what he really thought about me. Probably that I was brazen and spoiled. I didn't know what came over me to kiss him that way.

It didn't help at all to know I couldn't have him.

15.
Tom's Call
Tom

I suppose I should have been thinking about any number of things after that Christmas night, but what I couldn't get out of my mind was her kiss. I went about my chores trying not to remember how she felt and smelled, but instead it came back all the more vividly. To have her near me was all I wanted, yet when she was close I wanted to get away. What did she mean by kissing me that way?

We met in the barn a few days later, just by accident. There, she dropped a blow when out of the blue she said she'd end up marrying someone else. Well that meant she wasn't expecting to end up with me, didn't it? The only thing clear was that if Parsons found out we'd kissed, he'd fire me and I'd have to go back home.

"Tom, we was thinking of hitting town, maybe visiting the druggist on New Year's Eve," Shorty said as we rode in from checking cattle, the evening after Evie and I met in the barn. "The Parsonses will be visiting at the Kendricks ranch, and we won't be needed hereabouts. Time to celebrate our recovery. You game to join us?"

"You bet I am," I replied. I unsaddled Wanderer, fairly shaking. The news of Evie seeing Riley Kendricks over New Year's hit like a blow to the gut. I welcomed the chance to get away.

But a high cold wind on New Year's Eve put an end to our plans. The family left for the Kendricks ranch before it hit, but we three ranch hands had to stay huddled in the bunkhouse, trying to keep warm as the thermometer outside dipped to ten degrees and gusts howled around the eaves. I sat on the side of the bed, playing poker, in the very spot I'd sat Christmas night.

Jack and Shorty were in low spirits, having been cooped up all winter. But their mood was nothing compared to mine.

"Somethin's eatin' you, boy," Shorty said as he dealt to Jack and me. "Jack and I are sure sufferin' cabin fever, and Jack's got the dry mouth awful bad, but somethin' else got ahold of you."

"It's nothing," I said. "I wanted to get to town too."

"Two dollars," Jack said. We made the stakes high, playing with our night-out money.

"You got eyes for that gal in the big house, you best think again," Shorty said.

"See two and raise two. Why would you think that?" I asked, trying not to show how thunderstruck I was at his observation.

"We seen you dancin' with her," Jack said. "And then we didn't see you afterwards."

"Her papa and mama won't hold with any romancing from the help, no matter how much they like you," Shorty said. "And they like you, Tom. You want to get ahead in this country, you stay on Parsons's good side. Call."

"Call," Jack said.

"She isn't interested in me," I said.

"If you say so. Just watch yourself," Shorty replied. "It's your call."

It took a minute to realize he meant the card game. I wanted to ask him what he thought Evie meant by kissing me, but he'd told me all he could. I'd have to figure my way out of this on my own.

Because I cared about her. The thought of her with someone else told me this. It was one thing to lose my own happiness, and I didn't care about her land. But if she were unhappy, I'd surely have it out with someone like Riley Kendricks.

"Two pair," I said, scooping in the money. "So, do her parents marry her off to the highest bidder?" I tried to sound casual, focusing my eyes on the hand Shorty was dealing.

"It ain't like that," Jack said. "Cowpunchers don't have much to offer, to their way of thinkin'."

"We cross a lot of lines, livin' so close with them. Some lines, though, cain't be crossed," Shorty said.

16.
A Perfect Gentleman
Evie

Mama worried over what dress I'd wear New Year's Eve at the Kendrickses'. She stood in my room looking over my options, laid out on the bed—a red velvet, a blue calico, and my green Christmas velvet. "The red is awfully fancy for an informal gathering, but the blue might seem too plain. And everyone just saw you in your Christmas frock," she said.

Lordy how it sounded, to worry over a choice of dresses when some people didn't have anything to choose from!

This visit to the Kendrickses' was partly to

smooth over bad feelings. Mr. Kendricks had put up some fence on land my papa always used as range land. Kendricks apologized, but left it in place. My parents were going to pretend they weren't angry anymore, when in fact they were still upset. But they thought it best to get along with neighbors they had to depend on, and wait to change things later.

The reason I dreaded this visit was that it would remind the Kendrickses that I was eligible for courting. And that Riley was suitable. Events hadn't gone as smoothly in that quarter at Christmas as my parents had hoped. Mama had grilled me about my disappearance on Christmas night. I'd said only that I felt faint and had gone to my room to lie down. Fortunately no one could contradict my story. But Mama grumbled that I hadn't spoken much to the gentlemen at dinner. She wanted me to be more sociable and less headstrong. She picked up on this theme again as she looked at my dresses.

"Be nice, Evie. Talk to Riley. He won't bite, you know."

"Well, I wish he would. At least that would be *something* interesting."

"Evie!"

"Mama, he's always been a boor. When we were kids, he'd just tease girls. Now, he just talks about hunting and fishing."

"Well, you could listen. Act like you're interested, for pity's sake. He may say something you like."

"He doesn't care about what I like."

"Most of the time, it's up to the woman to listen to what the man likes. That's just the way of the world, dear. You can't be always thinking about what *you* want. Here." She held the calico out to me. "It sets off your eyes."

The Kendricks house was a two-story farmhouse with the usual outbuildings, ten miles from the nearest town and ten miles from our place. By the time we arrived for dinner, the wind was howling fiercely and the temperature was dropping. But the house was warm and gaily lit, and beautiful inside. Mrs. Kendricks was from an old Kentucky family and she'd brought fine furniture west with her. Mama sometimes felt like a plain German housewife next to Mrs. Kendricks, but they both liked to laugh and had great fun together.

The big dining room sparkled with crystal and china. We had onion soup, venison and beef steak, potatoes, beets and turnips, fresh rolls, and bourbon chocolate cake for dessert. That was the only hint of liquor, because the Kendrickses didn't hold with drinking any more than my parents did.

After dinner we went into the parlor, and Mrs. Kendricks played the piano while we sang her favorites, "My Old Kentucky Home" and "Old Folks at Home." Then Anna and Guy were sent to bed. Mr. Kendricks challenged Papa to a game of chess, Mama and Mrs. Kendricks got out their crocheting, and Riley and Chester and I looked at issues of *Golden Days for Boys and Girls*. Riley boasted to Chester of the deer he'd shot that week.

"Hard to find deer around here," Chester remarked.

"We knew there was a group wintering down by the river. Went out there at night, Papa and me, shined a lantern in their eyes, took three of them easy as pie."

"Isn't that unfair to the deer to shoot that way? They never have a chance," I said.

"Unfair to deer? They're just animals."

"But you should give them a sporting chance."

"Look, I don't care what you think of my hunting practices. It puts meat on the table, don't it?"

"Since when do you have to worry about putting meat on the table?"

That was as much acting interested as I could stand. I left the parlor and wandered around the first floor, lingering in the small library. The books there were mostly Greek and Latin classics and a number of religious volumes. They looked new and seldom used.

A little before midnight, Mama called me back to the parlor. Riley and Chester weren't around, but they soon showed up, Chester smiling in a lopsided way at me—they'd been drinking. I hoped Mama was too caught up in talking to notice. At the stroke of twelve, we blew out all the candles and lanterns and sang songs in the darkness. I was standing apart from the others. Riley sidled up next to me as we sang, too close, and the next thing I knew he pressed against my bosom! "Stop that!" I whispered, and pushed him away.

"Come on, Evie, give me a kiss."

"Leave me alone, Riley, or I'll tell your mama you're drunk."

"I'm supposed to be friendly to you. Come on. Be friendly."

"Go to blazes."

If I'd slapped him, Mama would have heard and investigated. But we were here to smooth away bad feelings, not create more. I just walked away.

Later, though, when we were in the guest room I shared with Anna, I told Mama what Riley had done.

"Oh no, Evie, you must be mistaken."

"No mistake. He said he wanted me to get friendly."

"Oh dear. Well, you did right. A lady has to let a gentleman know what the limits are."

"A gentleman doesn't try things like that with a lady, Mama. You taught me that."

"Well, he shouldn't. Some men will. But Riley's been well brought up, Evie. I'm sure he's sorry, and won't do that again. He's not a roughneck, you know."

"I think he'd been drinking."

"Oh no. The Kendrickses don't allow drinking."

"I'm pretty sure."

"Well, even if he was, his parents will put a stop to that kind of thing. He's a good boy, Evie. Just be firm, and you'll be all right."

We left soon after breakfast the next morning. I hadn't had to talk to Riley, and I was glad. I settled in the buggy, taking home something new: knowledge that Mama's rules, when it came to men and boys, were less than accurate. For example, I had gone into the bunkhouse with Tom, who turned out to be a perfect gentleman. Riley, the supposed perfect gentleman, on the other hand, was the one I had to look out for.

From here on out, I resolved to make my own rules.

The barn seemed to be the only place to "accidentally" meet up with Tom. The next day I watched, from my window. Even though it threatened to snow, I ran to take my pony out when he started his chores.

"Look, you probably think I'm always chasing after you," I began.

He turned toward me then, amused. "That was the furthest thing from my mind, Miss Parsons."

"Don't call me Miss Parsons. Please, Tom."

He was no longer amused. "What do you want, Evie?"

"I want to apologize."

"You already did."

"No, I mean, I learned, over New Year's, I've been wrong about some things."

"Wrong about what?"

"Wrong in thinking . . ." I didn't know how to tell him. He didn't look at me.

"I hope you enjoyed your time at the Kendrickses'," he said.

"Not at all. But I'm not marrying Riley Kendricks."

He looked at me then. "Why are you telling me this?"

"Because you're more of a gentleman than he'll ever be. I'm sorry I walked out on you in the bunkhouse."

"You were right to. I put you in a bad spot."

"I got scared of someone finding us. We'd catch hell, I'd never see you again, and you'd lose your job." I was blundering this. I looked right at him and said, "I don't want to hurt you."

He looked back at me, straight into my eyes, and said, "I don't want you to get hurt."

And right there I knew I loved him. And I knew he loved me back.

We didn't kiss, or hold hands, or do anything. We just let that new knowledge hang with the dust motes in the barn air between us.

I'd never thought much about falling in love. I guess I'd thought it would be dramatic, like in a fairy tale or tragic play. But it wasn't. I didn't fall anywhere. This connection to this other person was just there, quiet and sure. And joyous, like something I'd known all my life yet hadn't seen before.

I smiled at him, and he smiled back. He poked the broom at me, playfully, and said, "You'd best get back. You're interfering with my sweeping."

"Oh, am I? I've got things to do myself, to be sure." I laughed as I left the barn, and, walking back to the house, I caught myself humming a Virginia reel.

17.
Underground
Tom

I began the New Year the happiest I had ever been. For the first time I stopped thinking about leaving in the spring and instead tried to figure out how to live my life so it could include Evie someday. That wouldn't be easy on a cowboy's pay. The best I could think of was to keep working for Mr. Parsons and save my pitiful salary until I could buy my own place. In the meantime, I'd learn everything I could and get to be near the girl I cared for.

We had to be sneaky around her parents during her time home from school, acting like we weren't interested in each other. I surely didn't want to be the cause of trouble for her. But since I wasn't in the house much anymore and Jack and

Shorty were always around outside, we got desperate for a chance to be together. Finally, the day before her Christmas break ended, she made good on her promise to show me the tunnel.

The way she showed me was typical Evie. I was loading hay on a sled in the barn to haul to the cattle on the nearest range, because a snowstorm the night before had covered up the forage. Suddenly there she was.

I dropped my pitchfork, she startled me so. Jack and Shorty were clear at the back of the barn and didn't see her. "Where'd you come from?" I said.

"What kind of a greeting is that?" She smiled, took my hand, and pulled me over by the wall. There was an open trapdoor in the oak flooring. "Papa's opened the tunnel, because of the snow. Come see," she said.

I climbed down after her, checking to make sure that the others couldn't see us. The tunnel was brick-lined and high enough for a six-foot man to stand up straight. It was dark and cold, but at the end, what must have been about two hundred feet, I could see a faint grayness.

"Meet me here at midnight," she breathed. She kissed me and ran off, her footsteps echoing off the bricks.

Well, if sneaking out at midnight to meet a boy wouldn't get her in trouble, and myself as well, I didn't know what would. All day, driving the sled out on the range in more fitful snowfall, I fretted at the thought of the risk we'd be taking. The snow slowed me down, and I got back too late to talk her out of this harebrained idea. I thought about not showing up. But the thought of her down there alone in the middle of the night didn't satisfy me either. So I met her.

The entrance from the house was in the basement. She showed me two limestone blocks that were stacked one on top of the other to look like part of the basement wall, but weren't mortared in place. Mr. Parsons had pried them open so that he could get to the house from the barn and vice versa without tracking snow into Mrs. Parsons's kitchen. The tunnel's builder, Evie said, had come from up North somewhere, where blizzards and deep snows made tunnels like this necessary, although it snowed so little here they hardly ever needed to use it.

It was cold in that tunnel, hardly a setting for romance. But she'd brought a goose-down comforter, and we wrapped up together, and gradually this idea began to seem better and better.

After we'd snuggled awhile, I whispered, "Evie? What do you think the chance is . . ." Even our whispers echoed down the cold walls of the tunnel.

"Chance of getting caught eventually? Pretty good, I'd say."

"No, I mean . . . is there a chance of you and me being together?"

She would not have met me down here on a whim. She had to be thinking seriously. But she was not through school and I had no money. Yet if we got caught and didn't marry, there was the threat that scandal could ruin her. Never mind that we hadn't done anything scandalous—the very fact of her being down here with me at midnight was enough. None of those ranchers' sons would have anything to do with her.

I wished I could have met her normally. I wished I could have been one of those tall fellows from the neighboring ranches who sat beside her at Christmas dinner, and whom Mrs. Parsons beamed upon when she saw him near her daughter.

Evie said, "I aim to finish high school this year. And then they mean to marry me off. If I were to marry someone they didn't want me to, they wouldn't help me any, Tom. No land, no nothing. I have five cattle to my name. And a hope chest with a half-finished tablecloth."

"I don't have anything, Evie. I don't want to run off someone who could offer you everything."

"I don't want anything those fellows have to offer," she said.

"You deserve better than me," I said.

"Don't tell me what I deserve." She was silent a good while. "Anyway, I'm going to teach after I graduate. I don't want to, but I can save up money. I can buy me a piece of land."

"You'd buy a piece of land yourself?"

"Why not?"

"Well, women don't usually up and do something like that."

"That's what you're going to do, isn't it? Save your wages and buy land?"

"Yes, because I aim to have something to offer you."

"Why shouldn't I do the same?"

"I'd think you'd want to save your money so you and your husband could buy land together."

She was silent again. Then she said, "Look here. You know how I feel about you. I hadn't wanted to marry anyone, but I don't see as I can do without you. I have to make myself independent enough to marry whomever I choose. Teaching won't make me independent, by itself. The pay is low and I'd have to live with whatever family they put me with. I need a place on my own land, with my own herd."

I didn't see why she needed to go to all that trouble. But I kept my thoughts to myself. The main thing was that she wanted to be with me.

"It will be a few years before I save up enough," I said. "You think you can hold off your parents that long?"

"I think so, if I tell them I have my heart set on teaching. Mama always wanted to be a school-teacher, but she never got to. How did it happen that I can't tell them about the things my heart is really set on?"

"Maybe I shouldn't work here. Maybe it would be less risky if I worked for someone else."

She kissed me again. "Don't you dare think of leaving," she said.

18.
In the Storm
Tom

A blizzard hit the night of January 6, a few days after Evie left for school. I never heard the wind shriek and cry so, a protesting howl that sought to destroy us with its fury, given the chance. The sturdy bunkhouse walls might have been paper, the way they shook, and the cold tore right through. We kept the stove blazing. Looking out the window in the night was like looking at a blank—it was just gray in front of the window, closed in. I burrowed under extra blankets, cold still, but it wasn't the cold that kept me awake.

The next morning I rode west on the sled to get an idea of the damage. The prairie was a world changed to white, blotted out and featureless, and it took a while to get my bearings. The snow had drifted in odd patterns; four feet deep in some low areas, not quite covering the ground in a few high spots, as if the driving wind had scoured it. I found a dozen cattle sheltered among broken-limbed cottonwoods in the river bottom, hungry but fine. I dropped hay, chopped through the ice for them, and drove on, finding nothing other than an occasional tree with branches stripped from the force of the snow.

I pushed farther west than usual. Cresting a ridge past noon, I met a straight line of drifted snow with an unusual series of mounds along it, and then I saw red hide at the top of one mound and realized, with a sick feeling, what happened. Kendricks, last fall, had gone against the agreement of the cattlemen's association all the ranchers belonged to and had put up barbed wire fence on part of his range. About forty of our herd had been pushed by the blizzard winds until they came up against that fence. With nowhere to go, they were trapped by the blowing snow, and they piled up on top of each other against the fence and smothered. I pounded on the top carcasses, cleared snow away from their noses, but it was no use. They lay frozen.

Tom

All afternoon, I rode south along the fence line and found about a hundred frozen cattle stranded against the barbed wire. A half mile past the end of the fence, protected in a draw ringed with cedars, I found more of the herd, weak but alive and glad to see the hay sled.

As I fed the cattle, I saw the clouds in the north begin to pile, wisp on wisp, and I knew I was in for trouble. Another blizzard was coming. I pushed the Percherons as hard as I dared. I was about ten miles southwest of the ranch, and the sun was getting low.

I decided to follow the fence, or rather the tops of the fence posts sticking out of the snow. The fence ran north-south, out of my way, but it was the only bearing I'd have in the storm. The wind picked up, wailing, blowing the packed snow in swirling gusts.

The blizzard hit before I'd gone two more miles, blowing into us with a fierceness that drained the energy right out of me. Wind drove the snow sideways. Freezing air clawed at my lungs. The horses were already tired, and I had to get off and lead them, breaking the way. I floundered on, coughing. I didn't want anyone at the ranch worrying about me, or starting out in this storm to look for me.

Darkness fell then like someone had snuffed out a candle, and the full fury of the storm whipped my face. I couldn't feel my nose, fingers, or toes. Worse, I couldn't see the tops of the fence posts anymore and didn't know where I was headed.

A man could freeze to death in half an hour at those temperatures on the unprotected plain, even wrapped in a buffalo robe as I was, the warmest kind of covering. I had to figure out some kind of shelter and weather out the storm. I thought of turning the sled on its side and huddling behind it, but the wind was too strong. By some kind of luck just then I stumbled against one of the weird mounds of frozen cattle. It stood about five feet. The horses shied against getting close, but they were too exhausted to put up much fight, and I unhitched the sled and led them into the pocket of space protected from the wind by the barrier of the cattle. I burrowed down in the snow to get myself and the horses as much out of the wind as I could, and then huddled between the horses for warmth.

If the blizzard lasted, I would die. My shelter wasn't much of a shelter already and wouldn't protect me for long. If I died, my sister would never forgive my father. I hadn't forgiven my father, and I didn't want to die with anger still between us.

The blizzard drove snow over the horses and me, and I had to keep burrowing upward to clear an air hole. Cold fear gripped my stomach, but, strange to say, I wasn't really frightened for myself. What scared me most about my own death was the thought of bringing grief—to my sister, to my father, to Evie.

My shoulders cramped and my fingers stiffened. Belle and Lady were no longer restless; I didn't know how long it would be before they would freeze. But there was nothing more to do.

My head jerked up—I'd fallen asleep. I was choking—the air hole had blown shut. My lungs ached. I raised my arm, then realized I didn't know what was up or down. I started to tremble and couldn't stop myself. It was pitch dark. I struggled to rise, but my feet were numb. I flailed my arms until I hit snow and broke through, and the force of the cold air hit me like a shock. I bent to clear snow from the horses' nostrils, but they were clear, and the horses were breathing. The warmth of our bodies had created a thin snow cave in the drift. I touched the walls and found them icy from where our breath had met the snow.

Sometime later—I don't know how long it was—the voices of the wind in the storm stopped. I looked up through the air hole and saw stars. The storm had passed.

I poked my head out of the cave. The snow blotted out everything else to an eerie glowing grayness under the stars, and there was no moon.

I stood unsteadily on feet I still couldn't feel. I tried to rouse the team. Only Belle would stand. Lady was breathing, but her eyeballs had rolled back in her head. She wouldn't make it.

I dug us out as best I could, tramping down the snow hard enough for the horse to get out without struggling. The stomping didn't bring the feeling back to my feet. Ten feet away, the drift covering us diminished to bare ground.

Tops of fence posts still showed at intervals, and before long a glimmer in the east gave me more direction. I estimated distance by counting my steps. The counting kept me awake and focused. I dared not ride the horse—it stumbled as we walked. Except for the steady crunch of our steps, there was no noise, no birdcalls, no wind. An eerie quiet settled all around. The storm hadn't left much new snow, and as the sun rose I began to know where I was. The horse perked up, heading for home, and we were able to drag ourselves back to the ranch before noon, where we created a big stir that I took no notice of, because I passed out.

19.
The Aftermath
Tom

Don't tell Evie. That was the thought on my mind, but I couldn't speak it as Mrs. Parsons rubbed snow over my frozen feet, causing a pain that felt like a thousand hot needles sticking in me. If I said that, she'd want to know why not.

Mrs. Parsons saw me grimace. "Good, it hurts. That means the skin isn't dead. Your little toe don't look so good. Can you stand?"

Now I was the one in the sickroom, in nothing but my shirt. I made it to my feet but immediately fell back onto the cot set up beside the feather bed. "We'll try again later. Eat your soup. You're one lucky young man," she said as she carried the bucket of snow downstairs.

I lay on that cot for the better part of two days, alternately sleeping hard and hallucinating about voices in the wind, crying. Whenever I was awake, I was aware of someone in the room watching over me—Mrs. Parsons or Jack or Shorty. Once Mr. Parsons was there, even. Mrs. Parsons, bless her, took care of me constantly, bringing me soup and rubbing and wrapping my sore feet.

When my head cleared, I did some serious thinking. What if I had died? How could I cause someone so much pain? Maybe it would be better to get out of our romance now, before it got any deeper. The job I'd taken was dangerous and uncertain. It wasn't right to risk hurting her. Maybe this was why the cowboys I'd known weren't married.

The faces in Mr. Parsons's library the next morning were grim. Shorty and Jack stood stiffly on the Persian carpet, conscious even then of not dirtying it with their boots. My own boots hurt my feet too much to put on.

"Tom, we're glad you're with us, among the living," Mr. Parsons began. "When you didn't come home, we weren't so sure."

"Takes more than a little snow to get this feller down," Shorty said.

"Might have known he'd find a way to make himself comfortable out there." Jack grinned.

I stood in my socks and described my adventure. "The cattle couldn't make it to cover. The fence stopped them," I said.

Mr. Parsons leaned forward in his chair, and his hand hit the desk. "Damn Kendricks! We should have stopped him. A promise not to fence off access to the river isn't enough. Cattle country isn't made for fence." He was furious. "I'm going to ride him right out there and show him what it did."

"He can come out and help us skin those hides," Shorty said. "Only way we'll get any good out of them now."

"I'll make him bring his ax and chop those posts down!" Mr. Parsons declared.

"Jack and I never did find about two hundred head of cattle. That storm could have blown them anywheres," Shorty said.

"We have to know what our losses are. The papers are saying thousands of cattle have been lost across southwest Kansas," Parsons said. Shorty and Jack whistled.

"That's going to ruin many a rancher for sure," Jack said.

From the way Mr. Parsons glared at him, I could see that Jack had said the wrong thing. Parsons was worried that he'd be one of the ruined. I looked down at the carpet.

"Tom, I hope you're fit to ride now. As soon as this weather clears, I want you three to start counting," Parsons said.

"I'm all right," I said, although my head ached, my feet hurt from standing, and I wanted desperately to sit.

"You're going to have to ride farther than usual."

"You want us to take our axes along?" Jack asked.

Parsons grimaced. "I hope it won't come to that." He stood, indicating that our meeting was over. "I'm going to pay a visit to our neighbors, the Kendrickses."

Mr. Parsons returned the next day from his trip to the Kendricks ranch with a team of plow horses tied behind the buggy. "They're not Percherons," he said as we stabled them, "but until we can buy a teammate for old Belle," referring to the surviving team horse, "they'll have to do. Gentlemen, the fence remains. If it's still up in March, that's another story. We'll have to start the roundup early. The almanac predicts winter's end in eight weeks. That's when we'll go." He said no more about his meeting with Kendricks.

"We'll have to take an extra layer of bedding, starting so early," Shorty grumbled as we walked back to the bunkhouse. "Generally, roundup don't start till calving is over."

"What do we do?" I asked.

"We camp out on the range for nearly a month. That's why we'll freeze our tails, starting so early." He stopped abruptly and looked at me apologetically. "Sorry, Tom. You'll think I'm as green as money, hearin' me go on about freezing after what you been through. Anyway, we bring the cattle into camp so's we can look at their brands and count 'em. The other ranches have tallymen at our camp so's they can count their brands that we bring in and mark 'em off in their tally books. If a cow has a calf with her, we rope it and brand it. We also brand any strays we find—we call 'em mavericks. Then we mark 'em so's we know we counted 'em and move on to the next section. This time, we'll probably have to help calve too, some, 'cause the cows are weak. Hope you ain't got a weak stomach for blood."

The next day was sunny, with the temperature in the thirties. I eased into my boots, wincing at the pain, and Shorty and I took the new team out to the Kendricks fence line, where the cattle carcasses still lay under the snow. We skinned the thawing carcasses by cutting around the neck and legs, making a slit down the belly, tying the neck to one horse and the skin to the other, and riding in opposite directions. The hide just peeled off. I tired out early, partly from pain in my right foot, but the work went quickly, and we were able to get all hundred hides by the end of the day. We found the sled and Lady and my snow cave. I turned away so Shorty wouldn't see my face, because all of a sudden I was fighting back tears, and my weakness shamed me.

We loaded the hides on the sled, and one of the cow carcasses as well for a barbecue when we got back to the ranch. There was no way to save the rest of the meat, especially with the warm weather, so all we could do was wish the coyotes happy eating.

Because it was Friday and the weather mild, Evie and Chester were home for the weekend. For the first time since Christmas, I didn't look forward to seeing her, because I didn't want to talk about my ordeal. Luckily, there was no chance that night because Shorty and Jack and I stayed up late making roundup plans. Next morning, another clear, mild day, Chester helped me dig the barbecue pit and set up the roasting spit out behind the house. We talked some as we hacked at the semi-frozen ground, about the blizzard, about school. Then he stunned me by saying, "Evie's told me about you two."

Well, since he would have punched me if he'd objected, I just nodded. "I haven't done anything to hurt her."

"Well, see that you don't."

"I want to marry her someday, but your folks would put up a fuss," I said.

"You're right about that."

"I'm surprised she told you."

"She thought maybe I could help out. I aim to get married myself next year, to a town girl, only the folks don't know. They want me to take over the ranch, but I don't want it. Lila's father can set me up in the hardware business. I could have my own store someday. The folks wouldn't mind if I married her—they're not as particular about me as they are about Evie. But they'd sure mind me going into the hardware business—unless, of course, they had someone else to help them out with the ranch. Family, I mean." He glanced sideways at me to see if I understood.

I did. There was the temptation of the ranch again.

Chester had Evie's knack of thinking plans through. He was aching to be on his own, I could see. He had missed school often because of illness when he was younger, and it was hard on him, two years older than Evie, to still be a schoolboy.

"I'm no Riley Kendricks," I said.

"Riley Kendricks wants to prospect for silver in Colorado this spring more than he wants Evie. And that's just as well."

It was fine with me that Chester wasn't keen on a match between his sister and Kendricks. I was relieved to know Riley would be out of the way, but there were still others more suitable than me.

"You wouldn't object if I married her?" I asked him.

"Heck no. You're all right. It's my parents who have the notions about who's best for her. Papa thinks you're a fine stockman already."

"You know, it's a funny thing." I paused, not knowing how much to confide in him. "Out there in that blizzard, I realized the one thing I didn't want was to give Evie cause to worry. A stockman has a dangerous life."

"Not the way my father ranches."

I chuckled at that. Mr. Parsons did his best work when he told others what to do. "I couldn't afford to hire all the work done, like he does," I said.

"Are you saying you don't want the ranch?"

I considered this. Ranch work appealed to me infinitely more than storekeeping, but farmwork, plowing and planting like my father did, for all its poverty, had its appeal too. I was less likely to get caught in a blizzard, for instance, less likely to get caught in a range feud like the one brewing with the Kendrickses over the fence. Besides, I was far from sure that Parsons would ever offer me his ranch.

"I'm not saying I want it. I'm not saying I don't," I said finally.

"Well, anyway, I'm for you. Course I won't say anything to anyone."

There didn't seem to be anything else to say after that, so we finished digging in silence. I felt less guilty, glad of an ally in the family, but at the same time more nervous, because someone else knew our secret.

Evie came out then. "Here's the hero of the

hour," she said. She'd already heard. Of course someone would have told her.

"If you call dragging in half dead heroic," I said.

"Better than all dead," she said lightly.

"Evie, I told him I knew about you two," Chester said.

"Chester," Evie said, "you are going to come in handy. Here I can stand and talk to Tom all day and Mama won't pay any mind as long as you're with us."

"Surely my idea of a good time is to stand around while you two ogle each other."

"Oh, go on then. How can I tell Tom my deep dark secrets when you're here, anyway?"

Chester left. Evie silently helped me finish setting up the roasting spit, two Y-shaped iron rods stuck at either end of the fire pit. A third straight rod with a handle on one end would be shoved through the beef, and either end would rest in the forks of the Y-shaped rods, so the beef could be turned as it roasted slowly over the fire.

"I'm glad he knows," I said finally.

"Good," she said. "He won't tell anyone, especially if he thinks it's in his best interest not to."

"He's all right."

"Yes, he is," she admitted. "Chafing at the bit,

like me, but all right. We've kind of looked out for each other, ever since our two brothers died when we were kids."

"I guess having somebody die on you changes everything."

She looked at me closely then. "Looks like you're planning to stay alive," she responded. "Mama told me all about it. Are you recovered?"

"My feet still hurt some. I may lose a toe." I said this casually, but her face got white.

"Does it hurt? Do you want to sit down?"

"It'd look funny if we were sitting together talking."

She folded her hands and looked at them. "Mama said you were out of your head for two days afterward."

"Not clear out of my head. I did some hard thinking, Evie. Maybe it's not right for you to get mixed up with me. I'll just cause you grief."

"You were clear out of your head if that's what you were thinking. I can handle grief." She said this lightly too, but with firmness, as if the thought had been on her mind as well. "Besides, I was more worried about my cattle."

"Worried about your cattle, were you? Well, that eases my mind."

"I might have worried about you some," she said. "Quite a bit, actually. But I might have known you'd survive. After all, you have me to come back to."

"I'm glad about that," I admitted. How I wanted to hold her then, right there where anyone could see us. We stood for a while awkwardly, not speaking. Finally she cleared her throat and smiled.

"Anyway, I really am worried about my cattle, Tom. If I've lost them, that sets us back a few years. Chester will go off and marry in the meantime and I'll never be free."

"If you really want to take a chance on me, then don't worry. We'll make it, Evie, with or without."

"I'll take that chance. But I want to know."

"None of the hides I skinned had your mark." Evie had her own brand, a sideways *E*.

"But Jack says you can't find two hundred head."

"We're going out on roundup early to see what the losses are."

"Tom," she said evenly, "I'm going too."

20.
A Change of Habit
Evie

To his credit, Tom didn't laugh at me when I told him I was going on roundup. But he didn't exactly cheer me on either.

"It's too dangerous for a woman" was his first remark.

"It's dangerous for anybody, but you're going."

"I have enough to do worrying about my own skin, Evie. I don't want to worry about yours too," he said. And then he smiled. He was thinking of my skin, I could tell, in a quite less-than-worried way. Still, he wasn't taking me seriously.

"I can take care of myself, Tom."

"But you don't have to go. We can find your cattle."

"But they're my cattle. Why shouldn't *I* take care of them?"

"Evie, this is crazy. You couldn't miss school."

"Why not? Chester's going. Anyway, I'm going to ask Papa."

I had asked Papa every year since I was twelve. Every year he said no. And every year I tried again. They were my cattle, my future. He had to understand my worry.

How could Tom not understand? I was counting heavily on those cattle. All of them were supposed to calve this year, which would double my holdings by the time I graduated. Plus I knew them, knew where to look for them.

Worry about Tom, after his narrow escape from the blizzard, was maybe the tiniest part of my desire to go. He'd proven he could take care of himself. But if I went along, I could keep an eye on him, even if he didn't want me there.

We hadn't settled this by the time I had to leave for school on Sunday. And we failed to settle it when I came home on the next few weekends. Frankly, the issue of whether I would go on roundup was not uppermost on either of our minds down there in the tunnel. Of course we had to snuggle against the cold, and naturally we had to smooch some. If I was sweet on Tom to start with, though, I only became more so when he honored me by not pressing for more "intimacies." We could have been more intimate and nobody would have been the wiser. And frankly intimacy was a big temptation to us both. But there was too much at stake, if we wanted to end up with a life together in the long run, and we both knew it.

So there was plenty of time for talking things over. I loved hearing him talk. And I loved the way he listened to my opinions. One night the talk turned to women in politics, a subject that was mentioned more and more often in the newspapers.

"What do you think of that movement to let Kansas women vote in city elections? We could have a woman city councillor or even mayor," I said.

"Well, that could work. Maybe a woman could clean up a town like she cleans up a house," Tom replied.

"Maybe. Some of the state senators think that giving women the vote would lead to their 'moral collapse'—I'm quoting what the papers said."

"Why would they think that?"

"I guess by exposing women to all those rough male politicians."

"Seems to me if women have to live by the same laws as men, they might as well have a say in making them."

Small wonder I was smitten with him.

Tom did lose his toe to the blizzard. The doctor came out and took it off one day while I was at school. When I got home that weekend, I made him show me his foot. It was his right little toe. But all I could see were bandages. "Is it sore?" I asked.

He nodded. "Feels odd to have a piece of me missing."

I stroked the bandage gently over the place where his toe should have been. "I wish it hadn't had to come off."

"If I had to lose something, a little toe is the thing. It could have been a foot or a whole leg."

"Or all of you." I shuddered.

"It's not so bad. There's parts I can do without and parts I can't." He winked at me slyly. "You, for instance. Rather lose a toe than you any day."

I'd rather hear sweet talk like that than reasons why I couldn't go on roundup, so I didn't bring the subject up again with him. But as the weeks went by with no sign of my cattle, I got more agitated and more determined to go. When I came home in February, I went into Papa's library in the evening, after he'd had a good dinner, and told him I was preparing to take my teaching certificate examination. This was to soften him up. Then I told him I wanted to go on roundup. I should have saved my breath.

"No daughter of mine is going to go out cohorting with a bunch of cowboys."

"I'm not going to do anything wrong!"

"It's not you I have to worry about, is it? Evie, they'll find your cattle without your help."

"Papa, I can ride as well as anyone. Better than Chester, and he's going."

"Chester needs to learn."

"Chester would look out for me."

"Evie, what would people think of you, out there among those roughnecks?"

"I don't care what people think."

"It's time you did."

"Other girls work cattle."

"Name one we'd have to dinner. Some might let their daughters ride around wild, but not your mother and me. It's not right."

"But Papa—"

"No."

First Tom, then my father. I fumed at the injustice. If I were a boy, there'd be no question about my going.

In town a few weeks later, I ran into Jack, recruiting cowboys for roundup at the drugstore. His breath smelled of whiskey and he had a flask in his pocket.

"Havin' trouble gettin' anyone to sign up," he grumbled. "I'll have to go into Wichita to look. Can't account for it. Usually there's more takers than work. I got only two on board, and they never rode cattle before."

"I'll ride with you," I volunteered. "You know I can handle cattle, and you won't have to pay me."

"That's true, and if you was a boy I'd hire you first thing. But, Miss Evie, you know your daddy'd pitch a fit if we took you on."

If I were a boy.

I don't know if I was serious at first or just wanted to see if I could get away with it. Both Chester and Miss Watkins were out, so I ran back to Miss Watkins's and took some of Chester's clothes and his hat out of his wardrobe. I had my own cowboy boots, but they were at home, so I borrowed a pair of his as well. I bided my time for an hour or so, until the sun cast shadows and Jack had had enough time to drain the whiskey flask and would be looking at the world through more of a haze than usual. Then I put on the clothes, stuffed my long braid up under the hat, and looked at myself in the mirror.

I didn't recognize myself. The loose jacket, pants, and hat were a little big, but someone who could have been a boy stood there staring back at me, slightly surprised. I looked like someone's younger brother who hadn't started shaving.

If I didn't recognize me, then maybe Jack wouldn't either. I took a deep breath and went out to see about a job.

Twenty minutes later I returned, took off the clothes and hat and boots, and put them back. Everything was back to normal.

Except that I, under the name of Caleb Hunter, was now on the payroll of the Parsons ranch.

21.
Ties That Bind
Tom

When Caleb's name showed up on Jack's duty roster, I figured it was time to pay a visit to my folks. Bad feelings had simmered between us for the better part of four months now, and it felt like a lifetime ago that I'd left. But in these short months my life had found some direction, and I could swallow my anger at them. The least I could do was assure them I'd look out for Caleb.

Because the Parsonses were religious, Sundays were free days, after the stock had been tended and services held in the parlor. So one sunny Sunday I saddled up and made the two-hour ride to Papa's. The place looked as cramped and weatherbeaten as ever. Papa emerged from the barn as I rode up.

"Well, look what the cat dragged in! You've grown a foot, I swear."

Emma came over a rise just then with the horses and plow. "Tom! Tom! Stay there! I'll be right in!" She dropped the lines and started running. "Mama, Tom's home!" She ran up to me and gave me a hug. She was thin even for Emma, and she'd grown as well. Her dress was too short, and threadbare. I hugged her fully back, sorry for how much she still had to endure, living on this place every day. "So they've put you behind the plow now?"

She nodded, proud. "I can do sixty furrows in a day."

Papa said, "And come spring we'll find out how she is at planting."

Mattie appeared in the cabin door. "Come in, Tom, and rest yourself," she called.

It wasn't as awkward as I'd feared, this coming back. I had to duck at the doorway now, as Papa did. I sat down at the table and took off my hat, resting it precariously on my knees.

"How's Parsons been treating you?" my father asked, drawing up a chair.

"Fine. Just fine. How have you all been here?"

"No worse than usual."

But he and Mattie looked thinner. More lined and ragged too.

"Tom, would you like some water?" Mattie asked.

"Yes ma'am, that would taste good."

The conversation lapsed. We all watched Mattie fill a cup for me from the water pitcher.

"You all come through the winter with your shirts on?" Papa asked.

"Just about." I didn't feel like going into my blizzard story. "Parsons lost some cattle, though. Maybe quite a few."

"Can't say as I feel too sorry for him, even so. May do some good to bring him down a notch," Papa said.

I cleared my throat. "Well, ah . . . is Caleb around? That's what I've come about. Even though he's a might young for the roundup, you needn't worry. I'll look out for him."

Mattie let out a strangled sound. "He's with you?"

"No. His name is on the Parsons payroll to work spring roundup." Why would Mattie think he was with me?

"Thank God," Mattie said. "We heard he took off for Colorado."

"We haven't seen him for two weeks," Papa said. "A drifter come through, headed west, stayed the night, filled us all with stories about the riches for the taking in the silver mines west of Denver. The morning after he left, we woke up and Caleb was gone. No one has seen him. We figured he caught up with that drifter and headed west with him." He glanced at Mattie. "You reckon he changed his mind and come back?"

"I surely hope so," she breathed.

"His name showed up yesterday," I said. "I'll see what I can find out. Don't worry."

Of course Caleb would leave. There was not much to hold a person to that strip of earth, either in the way of comfort or kindness. With me gone, Caleb probably took the brunt of Papa's and Mattie's frustration, and now that he was gone Emma probably came in for it. No wonder she was glad to see me.

But Papa and Mattie were glad to see me too. They had missed me, and that was a shock. Even more of a shock was a suspicion that I had missed them as well. I didn't want to examine that notion too closely, but it made me pause. Maybe I just felt sorry for them, worried as they were about Caleb.

Tom

What explained these ties that bound us to place and kin, anyway?

"So," Papa said. "You're working roundup."

He was trying to find out if I'd be coming home, without asking me. Asking if I was coming home would be admitting something—need, maybe. He wouldn't try to force me, I realized— he didn't want to find out he couldn't make me return.

"Yes," I said.

But as I left, I made up my mind to send them money. Parsons already sent them part of my pay, as he'd agreed when he hired me. I resented every penny that went to them, figuring they owed me at least what they took. But now, seeing their raggedness and their loss, I decided to send more. The debt was one I could forgive.

22.
Confusion
Evie

Caleb Hunter's name was just the first that crossed my mind when Jack asked me for one, when he hired me. It would be useful, though. Tom would have to be on my side, have to play the part of the big brother. He would have to be in on my secret, as I couldn't fool him through the roundup. I probably couldn't fool Shorty either, or even keep fooling Jack. But I'd deal with them once I got out on the range.

I never even thought that Tom wouldn't go along with my plan. He'd objected to my going as a girl, but with my reputation protected by my disguise, what could he fuss about?

After school one day near the first of March, a few days after I'd hired on for the roundup, Miss Watkins asked me to help her get her flower beds ready for spring. I raked around the crocuses, which were already putting out green shoots, and pulled dead things out of the ground to make room for the seeds. I liked the feel of dirt under my hands, but my thoughts were surly. The flowers that she'd force to grow there would be boring, tame things, violets and daisies. Pretty enough, but if they got the nerve to blossom wherever they wanted, she'd tear them out by the roots.

My heart jumped when I saw Tom riding down the street. I'd never seen him come to town before, and I thought something had gone wrong on the ranch and he'd come to fetch me. He stopped by the yard and dismounted.

"Is anything the matter?"

"Hello to you too. Miss Watkins, nice to see you."

"Tom," Miss Watkins said primly.

"I'm in town on business, Miss Parsons, and your mother wanted me to bring this to you." He handed me a box filled with gingersnaps. I offered one to him and to Miss Watkins.

"What brings you to town, Tom?" I asked.

"I'm here to see my brother."

"I didn't realize your brother was living in town now."

"He signed on to work the roundup for us, and I want to speak with him about it. I'd best let you ladies get back to your flowers." He tipped his cowboy hat.

"Where's he staying?" I asked as Tom mounted his horse.

"I'm not sure of that myself," he said, smiling, but his eyes were faintly embarrassed.

He rode off without saying any more. Did he already know I'd signed Caleb's name, and this was some kind of code to tell me he knew? Suddenly I didn't think so. Tom never talked about his family, but I guessed I'd stumbled into some family trouble. I had to talk to him before Caleb did.

I mumbled something to Miss Watkins about giving Tom a message for my parents, and caught up with him as he passed the church. "I have to tell you something," I panted. "Can you stop?"

He nodded, and dismounted right there in the street. There were plenty of eyes that would see us together, and eyebrows that would raise if we tried to go someplace private, but maybe no one would think twice about our talking out on the dirt street in front of the Lord's house.

"About Caleb," I said. "Why are you looking for him?"

Tom flushed. "Evie, my family . . . You're asking for a long story here."

I'd never asked before. I knew from hearing my parents talk that Tom had a stepmother, that Caleb and Emma were his stepbrother and -sister, and that they were dirt poor. I'd never bothered to wonder about his life with them beyond that.

"I had to get away from my father's farm," Tom said now. Without thinking he took my hand, and I let it stay in his. "It wasn't just the work and lack of money. They took something from me they shouldn't have. They'd have taken my self-respect if I'd have let them." He gripped my hand, then dropped it suddenly, aware that eyes might be watching. "I'm sorry. Anyway, I guess Caleb felt the same way, because he's run off."

"Oh. Oh, I am sorry."

"My folks didn't know where he'd gone, and then his name showed up on our roster. Jack didn't know he was my brother and doesn't know where he's staying. So I aim to find him."

I'd put myself in the middle of a painful family mess! But I couldn't *not* tell him.

"Tom, Caleb didn't put his name on the roster."

"What do you mean?"

"I put it there."

"Evie, what is this?"

The look on his face told me just how sensitive a nerve I'd struck. I turned my head. "Tom, I was going to tell you. I planned to go on roundup by pretending to be Caleb. I even dressed like a boy. Jack had been drinking. He never guessed it was me. I swear I didn't know Caleb had run off."

"It was just a joke, then?"

"No, I'm going."

"You don't know where he is?"

"No."

He looked down at the dirt. "He's probably in Colorado. If he isn't dead. He's only thirteen. What am I supposed to say to my folks?" He looked at me then, accusingly.

"I don't know."

"Why did you even do it? You're messing with something you know nothing about, all for some harebrained notion of playing cowboy!"

"It's not a harebrained notion, and I'm not playing. You're not the only one who's been made to sacrifice." Unwanted tears filled my eyes at his words.

"Just leave it alone, this idea of going with us, will you?"

"No. I don't have to pretend to be your brother. But I have to go, Tom."

"I'll not help you, Evie."

He mounted his horse and rode off.

23.
The Mysterious Caleb Hunter

Tom

I shouldn't have gotten sore at Evie. I felt sick riding away from her. I didn't want to lose her. But any mention of my family bypassed my brain altogether and went straight to my gut. I'd begun to untangle that mess, but like a bad fishing line, it snarled again in a moment.

There was no point in looking for Caleb. Maybe he'd turn up before I had to tell my folks, although it was unlikely.

The only uncomplicated part of my life was getting ready for roundup, which I did with relief, cutting out horses to take, checking rope, unloading provisions for the chuck wagon, loading branding irons and firewood, packing gear according to

Shorty's advice. I worked eagerly, trying not to think of Evie. I didn't think she would go through with her plan, but even so, on the morning the new cowboys arrived and Jack called roll, when no one answered to Caleb Hunter, I was glad.

Evie's pinto pony was with us, though, as we rode to the first section of the range. We would check the range, about a ten-square-mile section a day, section by section, for new calves and stray cattle, branding any we found unbranded. Each cowboy needed several extra horses, which we drove along in a remuda. Chester was the wrangler in charge of this group. "This is the only part I like, working the horses," he told me as I rode up beside him. "The cattle can run to hell for all I care. They just end up dead on the table anyway."

"Chester, why is Evie's horse with us?"

He looked at me, then looked away. "She told me to bring him. He needs the experience." He dropped back to hurry along a horse that was lagging, and I didn't have a chance to ask him more.

We arrived at a good spot across the river, a shallow spot easy for the horses to ford, and made camp. It was only four in the afternoon, but we had to get up before dawn next morning.

After supper we sat by the fire. Jack had started

to lose his focus somehow during the meal, even though Parsons didn't allow liquor in his cowboy camps, so Shorty took over the job of giving us our instructions for the next day.

A rider approached from the north about then, and I knew who it was without even looking closely. She'd done it. She was dressed like a boy, in a boy's old pants, shirt, and hat, with her hair tucked up. Her pretty figure was hidden by a man's jacket, but she still sat a horse the same way, still cocked her head like Evie. She'd never get away with this.

I walked out to meet her. "You won't be able to pull this off," I said. It was too late for her to ride back home. She'd probably planned for that, so we'd have to let her stay.

"I won't be Caleb," she said. "I'll just be someone who shows up. I'll be my cousin Fred from Clearwater. You don't have to pretend to know me or have anything to do with me, and that way you won't get into trouble."

"Evie, you're being foolhardy. This is an awful risk."

She looked down at me coolly. "I thought you of all people would understand, Tom."

I stopped, stung. She rode on without looking back.

I followed as she trotted up to the fire, dismounted, and walked over to Jack. In a low voice that was anything but convincing to my ears she said, "Parsons sent me out. I'm to ride with you."

This was so like Evie, direct and without preamble, that I was sure Jack would recognize her on the spot. He did indeed recognize her.

"Why, here's Caleb Hunter," he said. "Tom, it appears we found your brother."

How could he recognize someone he knew when drunk, but not someone he knew when sober? But here was my chance to put a stop to the whole affair, to expose Evie and send her home in the morning. I might even win points with Mr. Parsons for protecting his daughter. I stepped up to the fire.

"That's right," I said. "Papa wouldn't turn him loose from his chores till now. Hope you don't hold this late start against him."

"Naw, we ain't done nothing but eat yet. You had supper, junior?" Jack got the cook to fix a plate. I noticed Shorty watching "Caleb" curiously. Chester was trying not to laugh.

I sighed. I wouldn't embarrass her here. Later, I'd get her to go back home. No one would ever need know she'd done this.

24.
One of the Boys
Evie

I could have kissed Tom, only that would have given me away right off. I smiled at him, but quickly put a frown on my face, trying to look tough as Chester led me past the others to the remuda. Chester whispered, "I'm going to bust a gut, watching you. I wouldn't have missed this."

"Hush up, will you? You don't even know me."

Andromeda ran up to greet me at the makeshift rope corral, but nobody noticed.

The food was good—bacon, baked beans, corn bread, and strong coffee. "Don't balance your plate on your knees," Tom stage-whispered as he walked by where I sat at the campfire. I grabbed my plate with one hand, moved my knees apart, and hunched forward. Much more manly.

There were eleven men including the cook, and luckily I didn't know any of them except for my brother and our three hands. None of the boys I went to school with hired out. Chester started up a card game with four of the others. Mama didn't hold with card playing, but Chester had picked up the wicked habit somewhere. I'd never seen him break a rule—not a big one, that is. We broke the little ones all the time, but knew when to draw the line. Tonight, under the open sky, the line had shifted.

I wandered over to the game after I'd scrubbed my empty plate with sand, dipped it in the bucket, and handed it back to the cook. The cards had shapes on them—red diamonds and hearts, black marks that looked like clover and upside-down hearts. Some had fancy people. I couldn't make any sense of them. "Call," the men would say, or "Raise," and then they'd put money in. Sometimes, from the look on a man's face, I could tell he was lying, but I couldn't get the hang of the game, even though I watched carefully.

"Royal flush beats two of a kind any day," Chester said, and he laughed and scooped up the cash. Mama would have skinned Chester if she'd seen him gambling.

I looked past the card players. One cowboy was reading, one writing a letter, and the regular Parsons hands, including Tom, were at the chuck wagon talking to the cook. Tom stood with his back to me.

Chester spotted me watching. "Hey, boy! Join us!" The smirk on his face said, *I dare you.* "What did you say your name was?"

So amusing, that Chester. I forced a smile. "Caleb Hunter. Sorry, but I've no money."

"Here, I'll lend you some. You know how to play, don't you?" He knew good and well that I didn't. "No? Well, here." He was remarkably deft at shuffling and dealing, for someone who wasn't supposed to play cards.

I learned about spades, clubs, kings, queens, and jacks, how to count the number of shapes on the card to find its value, and how to put together flushes, full houses, and straights. I also learned about the other players: Caesar from west Texas, whose brother Juan was the one writing a letter home; Whit, from Wichita; Vernon, also from Wichita; and Martin and Harry from England, two friends who wanted to visit the American

West after seeing Buffalo Bill's Wild West Show in London. They'd read about playing poker around a cowboy campfire and now couldn't believe they were actually doing it.

All of the hands were young, not more than twenty-five, and only Caesar and Vernon had cowboyed before.

I almost told the Englishmen that my father was from England, but then remembered who I was supposed to be. Chester seemed to have forgotten he had a father—I suppose he didn't want to be the boss's son to the cowboys. Papa would never have come to America on the strength of something so silly as a show or a book, would he? I wondered.

"Oh, I've always lived around here," I said when they asked me. True for me, and I guessed true for Caleb Hunter as well. I had no idea where he came from before his mother married Tom's father.

"Well, I suppose you've grown up roping and branding. We"—Harry included Martin in his gesture—"learned how to ride a horse with a stock saddle a month ago, and we've practiced roping since we contracted for this roundup, but we've much to learn." Caesar and Vernon exchanged glances.

"I, uh . . . I'm from a farm. Small herd. We fence the cattle, we don't rope or brand much." I hoped that would do for an excuse—I certainly couldn't tell them the truth, that I hadn't been allowed to learn these skills. A small knot of anger tightened in my stomach. Chester had grown up in the same place I had, and he could rope and brand, although he wasn't very good at either.

The card game broke up before I'd finished a hand. At Shorty's prompting Jack ordered us all to bed. "Bed? It's not yet seven," Martin complained.

"You'll roll your butt out of bed at four tomorrow morning," Jack replied. "You'll be thankful enough for your bed then."

I shivered, partly because of the cool night air, partly because I had a problem—how to answer nature's call. The cowboys had slipped off alone outside the firelight, but I couldn't risk being caught by one of them. Men had an unfairly convenient advantage when relieving themselves. I decided to wait until it was clear dark and everyone slept. So I waited anxiously as we unrolled canvas and blankets and settled in.

"Aren't you going to stretch out by your brother?" Shorty asked when he saw me carrying my bedding off by myself.

"Don't want the firelight and the snoring to keep me awake," I said.

He looked at me funny, but I just said, "G'night," and plopped down on my blankets.

Now that I was actually here, I wondered what I'd done. I tried to remember why I wanted to be here so badly. There was no real necessity. Tom had been right—the cowboys could handle my cattle for me. All I knew was that from the time I could remember, I had wanted to ride with the cowboys. And from the time I could remember, it had chafed me that I wasn't allowed.

So what if I did get caught? Running away to work cattle wasn't the worst sin a girl could commit.

I thought I'd burst, waiting. It was an agonizing time before everyone got quiet and dark gave me cover. Finally, I took my chance, slipping past the firelight and down to the trees that grew along the riverbank. When I squatted down, I couldn't see the firelight at all.

What a relief! But just as I was buttoning up I heard footsteps. The night was dark, moonless. "Who's there?" I whispered. My parents' warnings about wild cowboys flashed through my mind.

"Evie?" It was Tom.

"Tom, stay there."

"What? Wh—oh." I heard his footsteps stop.

"Just a bit." I smoothed my clothes and headed toward his voice. He was closer than I thought, and I bumped into him, hard. He grabbed me and held me tight. "Evie. You shouldn't have come here."

As good as his arms felt, I pulled away. "You didn't think I'd do it."

"Come on. We'll tell them you've gotten sick and you have to go back."

"No. This is more fun than I've had in my life."

"I saw you having your fun, playing poker. Your mother would tan your hide. You think we're out here just for fun?"

"Of course not. You know why I'm out here."

"I thought I did. I didn't think you'd go wild."

"That wasn't wild. I didn't even finish a hand. Look, Tom, I have to blend in."

He stood silently, fuming. "I'm not going to cover for you again. Or help you. How are you going to manage your, er, female necessities? You ever think of that?"

"I'll manage. I just finished managing."

I could feel him blush. "Look, you shouldn't be here. The work's too dangerous. I don't know

164

these men. They could be dangerous. You shouldn't be out here in the dark with them. Come on. I'm taking you home."

"No. You think you know what's best for me, my parents think they know what's best. If I let everyone tell me what's best, how am I ever supposed to know what's best for myself?"

"Sometimes you have to trust the people that care about you."

"And sometimes they have to trust me."

"I'm getting your horse. Dark or not, you've got to get out of here." He started toward the remuda.

What if I lost Tom because of this? That thought alone was enough to send me back. Something hardheaded in me, though, told me if I backed down, if I did what he and everyone else wanted, I'd never have him or anything else I wanted.

I went back to my blankets on the ground. He wouldn't dare pull me out of there with everyone around. I wished I'd put my bedding down a little closer to the others.

He came back. "I've saddled our horses. Come on, now."

"I'm not moving."

He tried to pick me up then. I struggled to get away.

"Everything all right over there?" We froze. Jack was headed toward us.

"He doesn't want to leave. But he's been vomiting. Might make the whole camp sick," Tom said.

"I ain't worried about that. He ought to stay, 'cause we're shorthanded as it is. I've worked a sick camp before. They get better by and by. You two just need to get settled so's the rest of us can sleep, you hear me?"

I glared at Tom. "Leave me alone," I whispered.

"Jack," Tom said in a low voice, "this is Evie here. She tricked you into thinking she was Caleb so you'd hire her. You hired her, Jack. Now you've got to help me get her back. Don't tell anyone, or we'll lose our jobs."

Jack wandered closer, and his eyes focused on me. "Miss Evie? Why the hell—er, 'scuse my language, but you shouldn't be here. Tom's right. We got to get you back home."

I whispered, "Jack, we've always gotten along fine, haven't we? But if you tell on me, I'll tell Papa how drunk you were when you hired me. You'll lose your job for sure, the way Papa is about liquor.

If you let me stay, no one else has to know about me, and everything will be fine."

What good was privilege if you didn't use it? Even so, I felt mean threatening Jack.

"What's all the ruckus? You're wakin' up the camp." Shorty had come to check on us.

"Caleb here is sick and needs to go home," Tom said.

"Except that ain't Caleb, that's Miss Evie, and she's going to get me fired," Jack said. Tom and I both glared at him.

"What the hell—pardon me, Miss Evie—but I thought that looked like you! What are you doin' out here? Your parents will skin you alive."

"She shouldn't be out here sleeping on the ground with men, and all of us roughnecks or coloreds or foreigners," Jack said.

"Evie was just leaving," Tom said.

"No I'm not. And nobody else needs to know, and that way nobody gets fired."

"What did you tell your folks?" Shorty asked.

"That I'm teaching school in Bluff City."

Shorty shook his head. "Chester know?"

"Yes, but he's not telling."

"How come he'd help you?"

"He doesn't care about the ranch. He wants me to help him marry his sweetheart, Lila, so this is a fair trade. He helps me, I help him."

"He'd tell on us, though," Shorty said.

"Not if he thought you didn't know."

"If you got in trouble, he'd blame us."

They knew my brother too well. "Look," I said, "two of you would have to take me back, because it wouldn't be proper to send me off with just one of you. Then you'd have to explain to my father what happened, and that could take the rest of the night. And I don't know how he'd react. He might fire you even though you brought me back, just because you had me out here in the first place. And even if he didn't, you wouldn't get back till daybreak, and then what good would you be working tomorrow? Let's all just get some sleep, and we'll sort it out in the morning." That would give me time to come up with a better plan.

"Your father's too fair to fire us for bringing you home," Shorty said. "And I been out all night before and worked fine the next day. You can't be out here with these men."

"These men don't know I'm a girl. And they won't find out if you don't tell them."

"That hat flies off, they'll know soon enough," Jack said.

"No they won't." I took off my hat and revealed the biggest cost. I'd cut my hair.

25.
Branding
Evie

〜o〜

We were wakened at four, as Jack had promised, by the cook ringing a bell that signaled breakfast. I was stiff, but had no trouble getting up—I'd slept light. Breakfast was good too—flapjacks with syrup. Why did everyone always complain about chuck-wagon food at the ranch?

When I took off my hat the night before, I'd killed the debate over taking me back. The men were too shocked, I think, to argue more, and they'd just murmured their wonder at what I was coming to. About my staying, Jack said only, "I'll swear I wasn't never drunk, never knew it was you."

"First sign of trouble, you're off to home faster'n you can spit," said Shorty.

Tom looked at me as if he didn't know me.

In the wee hours of the new day, the trouble of the night before faded, and my excitement took over. I'd never been out on the prairie that early, long before the sun was up. In the dark, the smell of wood smoke was welcoming, and the chill in the air stirred me. No bird noises broke the quiet, and the men spoke in hushed tones. I tried not to mind that Tom ignored me all through breakfast, or that Shorty and Jack kept their distance.

After breakfast we mounted our horses and "threw the circle." That was what they called fanning out in a circle, like spokes on a wheel, with the wagon at the center. We rode out from the center until dawn, maybe five miles, then turned around and came back. Out so far from the ranch, the land became rough, rolling. I stopped on a ridge to watch the sun rise. The meadowlarks and mourning doves announced its coming first with their twitterings and coos. Next, the sky turned gray, and gray topped the swells, which all of a sudden turned gold, and the depths became shadows. Then the sun was clear of the eastern rim. The land came into hazy blue focus. I'd seen a thousand prairie sunrises, and the beautiful change always filled me with hope, but today the hope lingered.

Branding

We searched out all the grassy hollows and watering places along the way and drove any cattle we found toward the wagon. That way we collected all the cattle within a circle ten miles in diameter. For an experienced rider like me, this wasn't hard. I coaxed a few cattle out of a draw just by riding in the direction opposite the one I wanted them to go. The calves followed their mothers and I followed along in the rear. The day grew warm and for the first time I felt all right about cutting off my hair. There was no heavy mass of it on the back of my head making me sweat.

I'd almost cried when I'd cut it. On the day before roundup, Chester had fetched me from Miss Watkins, who thought I was leaving to teach school. A week earlier, I had taken my examination and passed, earning a teaching certificate without graduating. Both Miss Watkins and my parents thought that I was finishing up a term for a teacher over in Bluff City, and I'd live with a family there. My mother was proud of me, and in the flurry of roundup preparations nobody asked many questions. I wouldn't be expected home till the end of the school term. By then roundup would be over and my hair would have grown some. I could always tell my parents that some crazy Bluff City girl had talked me into a new fashion.

So, on the day of roundup, I packed a trunk and dressed in my best dress. My father drove me in the carriage to the train depot where I would catch the train to Bluff City. He unloaded the trunk and then stood next to me, his thumbs hooked in his vest.

"You don't have to wait with me. The train will be along any time now," I said. I counted on his being too busy to wait with me, but he said, "I'll stay, to make sure you depart safely."

"But you're busy with roundup. You should get back home."

"I don't want to worry about you. You've never been so far from us before, among strangers," he said.

So I bought my ticket, stowed my trunk, and hopped aboard the train to Bluff City, waving at the door of the train car. I walked the length of the coach, and, while my father scanned the windows looking for me, exited out the back. I hid in the station until the train left and my father drove away. Then I went to the livery stable and picked up a horse Chester had left for me from our remuda. My cowboy gear was packed in a carpet bag that I took with me out of town.

A mile or so out of town, I changed clothes. I pulled my braid over my shoulder, took my sewing scissors out of my bag, and cut. My hair came off in one long swatch, which I looked at for a time and then buried on the prairie.

Soon I met up with Whit and then Martin and Vernon, all driving the cattle they'd found, and then eventually all the rest, and we brought our combined herds back together by about ten o'clock. Then we ate dinner, half of us at a time, while the other half held the herd. After dinner some of the cowboys rode out again, while the rest of us branded calves.

The branded cattle were from three different ranches. At the wagon, Jack and Shorty would mark all the new calves with their mother's brand. Tallymen from the other two ranches rode up to count the cattle with their brands and enter the number in their tally books. None of the cattle had my mark.

Then the branding started. I watched from my perch on Andromeda at the edge of the herd. Shorty and Jack cut out a calf and drove it toward the branding fire. Riding on either side of the calf, they swung their lassos and let go, one toward the heels and one toward the head. Their horses stopped short the instant they felt the pull of the rope, and the calf flipped down, stunned. Shorty jumped off his horse, raced to the calf, and bound its hooves in a flash. Tom ran over with a hot iron and seared the brand into its rump. The calf bellowed with pain, and the flesh sizzled, letting off acrid smoke. "You got it too deep. Not so hard next time," Shorty called. One of the new cowboys, Whit, ran over and brushed a salve on the new brand to help it heal, then Shorty and Jack loosened the ropes and the calf bolted back to its anxious mother.

As soon as the branding was done, the cook rang the bell for supper, even though it was only four o'clock. We ate quietly, tired out. But after supper we helped the cook pack up, loaded our things on our horses, and headed for the next camp, about ten miles along the river.

We did this day after day. I was surprised to find that keeping my secret was easy. Part of it was that I was alone a good deal, searching for cattle. Also, most of the hands were new, and no better at cowboying than I was. They left the branding and roping to those with experience, so no one ever questioned my ability. At night we were too tired for much talking. Shorty sometimes played his fiddle, or Whit his guitar. The hands broke out the cards only a few times, and I didn't join them again. The only opportunities for talking were at meals, and I made sure to keep my mouth full.

But part of the reason I could keep my secret was that those who didn't know me just saw what they expected to see—a cowboy. It never occurred to them that I might be something different.

"What happens to cattle we don't find?" I asked Shorty one morning as we were herding cattle back toward the branding fire. Shorty, I had discovered, was someone who knew everything there was to know about cattle.

"The calves don't get branded. They wander free, and then next year, when they're weaned from their mamas, nobody knows what herd they belong to. They're called mavericks then, and anybody who finds them can brand them and count them on their tally. That's why we got to find all we can."

Mavericks, free without a brand, belonged to nobody. That appealed to me—as long as they weren't mine. But the trouble was, they only counted if they had a brand.

One afternoon, I was off by myself, on foot, tossing my rope at the chuck wagon, when a calf broke away from the branding fire. He dashed among the cowboys. They hooted and hollered to make him head back, but that confused him all the more. He tore past the chuck wagon, and I threw the lasso on him, quick as I could. To my astonishment, I roped his neck. But I forgot to brace the rope with my waist and lean back, and the calf pulled the rope through my hands. I held on, and he dragged me about twelve feet before I thought to let go.

By that time Shorty was after him on horseback and roped him. I stood, rubbing my blistered hands together. Tom came running toward me. "You all right?"

I nodded.

"Wear your gloves, and plant your feet. Didn't you have sense to drop the rope?"

"I roped him though, didn't I?"

"Come on, let's get some salve on those hands."

Tom was even angrier with me now. I could tell he was by his silence as he salved my blisters. I'd skinned my knees and elbows too, and torn holes in my pants and shirt. He helped me wash off, but stayed silent as the cowboys teased me about my mishap. Shorty and Jack didn't tease either. No doubt they were thinking about what would have happened if the boss's daughter had gotten herself seriously hurt.

What Tom thought about this misadventure he didn't say. He didn't speak to me at all that evening and rarely over the next few weeks. I'd wondered if it would be hard to be near him all the time, especially at night, and have to pretend not to be smitten with him. I needn't have worried. He stayed angry, and it wasn't hard to keep my distance.

I began to worry some about our future together. I worried even more as the roundup neared its end and we hadn't found any of my cattle.

The last week of the roundup, we rode the range close to the Kendricks spread. That first morning I spotted a young bull drinking at a creek and got near enough to him to see that he had no brand before he took off at a gallop. A maverick. I chased after him to tire him some. He disappeared over a swell. I crested it, and saw the bull running hard toward that terrible fence that had caused so much hardship. We were under strict orders not to tamper with it, because my father still didn't want trouble. But it was tempting to ride over and try to whack down a fencepost or two.

The bull veered and ran along the fence line. I galloped after him, riding hard to catch up. Never did I mean to scare him, but he was even wilder than the cows. He spooked when he saw me, and crashed into the barbed wire at a run, knocking down a post and leaving the fence snapped and sagging. And then he ran off, straight toward camp, limping wildly as he galloped. I found blood on the barbs of the damaged lines, and some hide.

My horse was tiring, but I pushed it on hard, to catch up. Now it was even more urgent to get the bull to camp, to see how badly it had been hurt.

The bull was tiring also. I kept a good space between us, but headed him off when he went the wrong way, and criss-crossing back and forth, we reached camp.

They could tell he was injured as he approached. Shorty and Vernon roped him and threw him, and Chester put the brand on. The cowboys crowded around to inspect the damage, me among them. Suddenly the rope around the bull's feet broke. We all backed out of the way fast. He leaped to his feet, lowered his head, and ran straight at me. I froze. A blow knocked me to the ground, but it wasn't the bull. "Stay down!" Tom yelled.

He'd ridden into camp, and, seeing the bull charge, raced to put his horse between the bull and me. His horse had knocked me down and turned the bull away from me. But the bull headed right for Chester. "Drop!" Shorty yelled. Chester crumpled into a ball in the dirt and covered his head. The bull leaped nimbly over him, his hooves missing Chester's head by inches. The bull jumped through the camp, knocking cooking pans and water pails, and the men ran for cover until Tom chased it away.

"Well, let him go," Shorty said. "He's cut up and he's lost some blood, but nothing to do for it. He might make it yet."

"He knocked down part of Kendricks's fence," I said.

"Smart bull," Shorty said.

The bull's charge made me think twice about facing the cattle the next morning. But when it came time to throw the circle, I went.

Shortly after sunup, on the side of a grassy hill, I came across a cow lying down. She let me ride right up to her. Usually cattle would run off at my approach. But she just eyed me, and I realized she was in pain. More than pain. She was in labor. Her sides heaved and red membranes oozed from under her tail. Her brand was a sideways *E*—one of mine!

I dismounted and checked her over. She looked weak and tired, as if this had been going on for some time. I stroked her neck, spoke soothingly so that she wouldn't be afraid of me. The morning was cool, with a gentle breeze, but even so her flanks were sweaty. It was hard to just sit there and wait for her. I walked up to the top of the rise to scout for anyone who could come to help me, but saw no one. I walked back to her and sat down cross-legged by her tail.

She bellowed each time her sides heaved with the labor contractions. When a cow is lying down, she should deliver within the hour—usually. But I waited with her until the sun was high, and nothing happened. If the cow was in labor too long, both she and the calf could die. I'd never helped birth a calf. Taking a deep breath, I started to reach inside her with my gloved hand, thought better of it, pulled off my glove, and stuck my bare hand inside under her tail. There was one hoof, but I should have felt two, and a nose—usually the forelegs and nose come out first. Maybe one of the legs was caught inside.

Never had I wanted to see another human so badly. If I hadn't come on the roundup, maybe a real cowboy would be doing this job, and maybe the cow would have a chance. But it did no good to think this way. I pushed farther inside, past the nose. By this time my whole arm was inside the cow. Sure enough, the other foreleg was tucked up under the calf. I tried to move it forward, gently, and pulled. Every time the cow bellowed I pulled, and when she was resting I tried to position the calf better. Each moan the cow made became weaker. Her muscles clamped around my arm so tightly it ached.

Finally, its leg straightened, and at the next contraction the calf moved forward. I kept pulling, although my arm was trembling with tiredness. The hooves emerged little by little. The calf's nose appeared, and then the rest of the calf slid out. My whole arm was covered in warm red goo. I undid my bandanna and wiped mucus from the calf's nostrils and mouth. It was a boy! He made a low bleat, but didn't move. The mother was too tired to notice.

I picked up the calf and laid him under the mother's nose. Neither animal moved. I rubbed them both, not knowing what else to do. The three of us waited, exhausted.

At last, the cow roused herself and began to lick her calf from one end to the other, and he raised his head.

I sat with them for another hour or so, until the afterbirth passed and the calf was nursing from his mother's udder. A strange pride swelled within me. This was a new creation, and nobody could tell me not to take part in it.

26.

The Flood

Tom

After weeks of fine weather the rain hit, pounding us for three days straight. Our clothes were mud, our bedding was mud, our hair was mud, our horses were mud. That was the good news.

We weren't finding much more cattle. The totals in the tally books were low, too low, so we stayed longer than we should have in some camps, hoping we'd missed a herd, but we hadn't. On the next-to-last day of the roundup, when the sun finally broke through, the books showed too many cattle still unaccounted for.

We threw the last circle, searching carefully, but still came up nearly empty-handed. There were calves, though, among the cattle we found, and we had branding work to catch up on. We branded calves until it got too dark to say for sure which calf belonged to which cow, and then we started again at first light. By midmorning the last calf was branded, and the last count made.

More bad news then. Mr. Parsons showed up to collect the tally books. He drove out in his light rig, behind Dante and Faust, and they had a hard time of it on the muddy ground. They arrived mud-covered, like the rest of us. I looked over at Evie, who was trying her hand at branding. She'd seen him. I couldn't tell what she thought. She was soot-covered as well as muddy, almost unrecognizable. That was just as well. She'd gone this long without being discovered.

My heart had been in my mouth at least once a day with her. Any fool could see how happy she was out here, and I had to admit she was as good as any of the new cowboys, maybe better than some. When the bull charged her, all I could think of was to protect her. Whatever foolishness she may have done, I wanted her to be safe.

Mr. Parsons barely glanced at the cowboys anyway. He was interested only in the sad story the tally books told. One hundred ninety-five cattle lost to the winter. Sixty-five new calves, less than half of what should have been. Only two of Evie's cattle had been found, a cow and its calf.

"Preposterous. How's a man supposed to make a living? And now Kendricks is claiming we've cut his fence and let his cattle out. We haven't, have we? I'll thrash the man that did it, as soon as I'm done giving Kendricks a thrashing."

Shorty said, "That fence was tore up by the bull. Ev—er, one of the boys saw him do it. Cut up the bull's leg pretty bad. It's Kendricks's fault."

"Which one of the boys witnessed this?"

Shorty froze. I said, "It was me, Mr. Parsons. I'll tell Kendricks what happened if you want."

"Testify is more likely. I hope it won't come to that, or worse. As long as the bull's blood is the only blood shed."

Parsons wasn't a man to swear at his bad fortune, or carry on, but he snapped at the least thing. He harangued Chester in front of everyone for the muddy shape of the horses, even though there was no way to avoid it. He upbraided Jack for not searching harder, for letting the equipment get muddy, for not hiring more men. Sometime during the day, Jack's movements began to get slower and his speech fuzzier. I never saw the man take a drink—I don't know how he sneaked his liquor.

At dinner, Parsons was angry about how much food we had left. He told Jack he'd bought too much. Maybe his anger distracted Parsons—he sat not twenty feet away from Evie and never noticed her. She was still sooty and muddy, and he was the kind of man who saw what he expected to see, not necessarily what was there. But I didn't know how he could not see his own daughter.

After dinner, we packed our gear in the chuck wagon and headed home. We had been out thirty-one days, and were tired and anxious to get back. I was particularly anxious that Evie not be near her father, and rode with her a ways behind the chuck wagon, which was behind everyone else.

We rode for some time without speaking. We hadn't spoken, except by necessity, for a month, even though we'd been around each other every day. Now it was hard to know what to say to her. She surprised me by speaking first. "Making sure Papa doesn't find out about me?"

"Yes."

"Don't worry, your jobs are safe."

"It's you I'm worried about. What kind of trouble would you be in if he found out?"

"I don't know. It's not the worst thing I could do."

We rode on. After a while, I said, "You know, sometimes I forgot you were Evie out there. You were a pretty fair cowhand."

She didn't say anything.

"Riding and roping, just like a man."

She turned to me. "Look, Tom, if you're trying to make me feel better, it's not working. I've lost my cattle, and I've lost you, in all likelihood. My father, who thinks I'm teaching school in Bluff City, is not two hundred yards away. And I already know I'm a pretty fair cowhand."

"Lost me? You haven't lost me. Irritated the blazes out of me, but once this is all behind us, things can get back to normal."

"And we can keep sneaking around as usual? I don't want to do that anymore either. I'm tired of hiding, tired of lying. I'm not going back to 'normal.'"

"What do you want me to do? Things back at your place haven't changed."

"No, but I've changed. I don't know how, but things are going to be different."

"Different between you and me?"

She eyed me. "If we got married, would you want me to help you work cattle?"

"I'd have thought you got that out of your system with this roundup."

"It's in my system more than ever now."

"Evie, look at you. You're dirty, and tired, and you about got killed out there. Is that the life you want?"

"I saved a calf out there. I rode the prairie every morning. Why wouldn't I want it?"

"Well, how would you manage the house and the garden, and you know, if we . . . if there were children, what would you do? If I needed you to help me, you'd do a fine job I'm sure, but I don't know that there would be the need." Instead of forgiving her for this stunt, I was becoming more upset.

"And would you want me to buy property?"

"But I don't see why you'd have to."

"No."

Whatever I'd said, it wasn't the right thing, I could tell.

"I can't buy any property anyway, now, with most of my cattle gone," she said.

"I don't see why this is so important," I said. "I'll save up enough, and then I'll marry you."

"Stop a minute," she said, and when we'd halted,

she continued. "You know I think the world of you, Tom. You're more than just somebody's ranch hand. I wish you thought of me as more than somebody's daughter."

"But I do," I said. "I don't care that you're Parsons's daughter. I've known you since you were twelve. The first time I met you, you were riding the prairie, wanting to go on roundup."

"And that's all right for little girls, but not for big girls?"

"We're grown up, we do what grown-ups do now. I don't understand why you're hanging on to a child's dream."

"No, you don't."

"Do you want to marry me, then, or keep chasing some fantasy?"

She was silent a moment. Then she said, "Why should I choose one or the other?"

"Evie . . ."

"Look, they're swimming the horses. We'd best help the others."

The cowboys, on horseback, were swimming the remuda of horses across the river. Shorty held Mr. Parsons's light buggy as it forded. Usually, the Chikaskia was a shallow, prairie river, about two feet deep at the ford, and narrow. But today the river was high in its banks from the rains, and swift. The chuck wagon, crossing next, became mired in the mud. Jack pushed the back end, while Evie and I helped push it into deeper water. The cook yelled for Jack to come lead the horses while he rode in the wagon, because he couldn't swim. Jack led the horses and the water buoyed the wagon bed up enough to keep it out of the mud, until they hit a deep channel in the middle. Suddenly Jack went under the horses, which panicked and floundered. The wagon went over.

I tore after the horses. Shorty ran in from the other side to help me. The cook grabbed for a line, but Jack had disappeared. We struggled to calm the horses, untangle them, and cut their harnesses. Then we swam them across to safety.

There was splashing behind me as I reached the opposite bank. It was Evie, pulling a half-drowned Jack to shore.

The other cowboys helped her stretch him out on the grassy bank. He wasn't breathing. Shorty pounded him on the back and he started coughing. Mr. Parsons was watching.

Evie was washed clean of the mud and soot now,

and her hat was off. Even with her hair cut short, there was no mistaking the color or the curl. And her wet clothes didn't hide her figure anymore.

Whistles of amazement exploded from the other cowboys.

Then someone cried out, "The wagon!" The river was carrying it away. It tilted to its side and came to rest on the opposite bank, about a quarter mile downstream. We ran to pull it out, all except Evie, Jack, and Mr. Parsons.

The wagon had stuck fast on a muddy bar, mostly out of the water but nearly on its side, and no amount of pushing was going to budge it. We spliced the harnesses back together in a makeshift way, tied ropes to the wagon and the harnesses, backed the team down the bank, and made the horses pull. We used sturdy tree branches as poles for leverage to prop the wagon bed after each pull, so that it wouldn't slide back into the river. Whit helped me position a branch and loosen the mud from a wagon wheel. "Was Caleb your sister, then?" he asked. "Did you know all along? That's mighty peculiar."

I didn't know how to answer him and keep Evie protected. "It's not so peculiar. She didn't think people would understand a girl cowboy."

"Why'd she do it? Who is she, anyway?"

These were the questions I'd been asking my-self for the better part of a month, and I wasn't sure I'd arrived at an answer. I said, "Look, she probably wouldn't want us poking into her busi-ness."

"Well, my sister herded cattle on the farm, before we lost it. Course, she was a little girl then, and we didn't have a choice. This girl must be pretty hard up for cash, or running away from a desperate situation. Maybe her kin have all died and she can survive by doing the only thing she knows. Maybe she dressed like a boy to protect her virtue, or so no one would ever know the depths she had stooped to."

He was starting to sound like the dime novels I used to read. "Maybe she just wanted to, and no one would let her," I said.

"Naw, women don't do things like that. I think you know, and you're not letting on."

"Here, give this wheel another shove," I said.

It took the rest of the afternoon to get the wagon free, and all that time I was frantic to be with Evie, to know what would happen to her. When Mr. Parsons joined us, Evie was nowhere in sight. Neither was Jack.

The sun was getting low when Mr. Parsons called the cowboys together to give them their pay. He called their names, handed them their money, told them they were welcome to come back for the fall roundup, and shook their hands. Then they were on their way. Except he didn't call Caleb Hunter's name, and he didn't call mine.

When the last of the roundup boys had left, Mr. Parsons turned to Chester, Shorty, and me and said, "Jack's been relieved of duty. When you get these horses in, Tom and Shorty, you may have the evening off. If there's nothing further, I'll go on ahead. One thing more. Shorty, I wish I could offer you the foreman's job now, but I don't know any men who'd work for a colored boss. Tom, you are now foreman."

Stunned, I didn't say anything as I watched him drive off. How could I be foreman when I'd only worked there five months and hadn't even been a permanent hand? By all rights Shorty should have had the job. He sat there on his horse, looking down at his saddle.

I cleared my throat. "I can't take this job. You know a hundred things more than I do."

Shorty sighed. "It's my dark face that's keeping me from being foreman. I thought Parsons would be different when I hired on, though. He said color didn't make no difference. And when Jack and I were so sick, they took us both right into their home, with their family. I don't know nobody else would have done that. How am I ever going to get married now?"

"Married?"

"Miss Emma Walker's been waiting for me for five years. She's in Dodge City now, and I been trying to get the money together to get her out of there, get a place of our own. I don't see how it's going to happen now."

I didn't know what to say. In Virginia, a colored boss would be an impossibility. But out here we'd all worked the same jobs and skin color hadn't made any difference. And Shorty was the best rider and roper I knew. He had already been more of a foreman than Jack, teaching the men and telling them their jobs, smoothing over disputes. He had done most of the planning for the roundup, had scouted the camps, had done the tally work on the books for the ranch. He must have been passed over once before, four years ago, when Luke left for Montana. The foreman's job should have gone to him then over Jack.

A selfish part of me realized that on a foreman's

pay I'd be able to marry Evie sooner, and maybe with Parsons's blessing, since a foreman had more status.

"I need a drink," Shorty said. "Let's go into town and celebrate Tom's new job."

Shorty and Chester and I drove the remuda to their range just east of the ranch, and then Shorty and I cleaned up at the bunkhouse. I stopped by the house to tell Parsons we'd brought the horses home, more as an excuse to look for Evie than anything else. I didn't see her, and of course Mr. Parsons said nothing about her. My hanging around looking for her would only raise suspicion and make matters worse for her. Chester had disappeared too, so there was nothing left to do but head for town.

It was about ten o'clock at night when we got there. Shorty led me around to the back of one of the drugstores and knocked at the door. The druggist came from the back room where he lived. "Hello, doc," Shorty said. "We're in need of some medicine—a quart apiece."

"Wait here," the druggist said. He went down to his cellar and brought back two bottles of homemade whiskey. "You boys don't cause any trouble, now," he said as we paid him.

"Tarantula juice," Shorty said as we headed over to the livery stable to drink. "He makes it himself down in that cellar among the spiders."

"Come on over and let's have us a party," said a voice from behind the livery stable when we got there. It was Jack. "You all celebratin' the new ranch boss?" he said, patting Shorty on the back.

"Naw, it ain't me. It's Tom over there," Shorty said.

"Well, I'll be hornswoggled." Jack looked from Shorty to me and back to Shorty. "Tom, is it?" Shorty nodded. "Well, Tom, let's drink to your swift rise in fortune." Jack raised his bottle. I looked down at my boots.

We sat on the ground, each with our own bottle. *Tarantula juice* was an apt name—the stuff certainly tasted like something from a spider. No one spoke for some time.

After a while, Jack said, "Could this happy promotion have been a result of your fortunate connection to a certain rancher's daughter?"

"How did you know about that?" I asked, startled.

"You think we didn't notice when you was out of the bunkhouse at night, or know why you was helpin' her out on the roundup?"

"We've done nothing improper, I swear. I aim to marry her. And her folks don't know about us, so that's not the reason he made me boss."

"Sure, boss, if you say so. Wonder what Daddy's going to do to her hide now. Why'd a gal want to up and ride with us anyhow? There's something peculiar there, now."

"Aw, Jack, let her alone. There's women that work cattle," Shorty said.

Jack said, "I know it. I knowed a woman in Texas, could work cattle with the best of us. But that was the way she growed up, and didn't have no other way to make a living. Miss Evie don't have to dirty her little fingers at all. She's playing at ranching like it's her toy."

"That's not it at all. She was raised riding and helping around the cattle," I said. "She's thought about this. She has her reasons." Reasons I didn't happen to agree with, but I couldn't let Jack run her down. "Jack, you should be glad more than anyone that she was along on that roundup."

"She should have let me drown, saved me the trouble of havin' the drink kill me. That's what I'm going to do now. Drown my sorrows."

We all fell silent after that, each of us in an ugly mood.

My stomach rebelled at the whiskey before I'd drained half the bottle, and I started retching. Shorty and Jack said nothing, but turned away, disgusted, as I leaned against the stable wall and vomited my insides out for nearly half an hour. Afterward, my sides and head ached. I lay on my back and stared up at the stars, let the cool night air wash over me. The thought of Evie flooded through me harder than ever then, and my fear of losing her got mixed up with my shock at Jack's leaving and my outrage over Shorty's injustice.

The stars looked down on me, remote and cold. I grew angry at how distant they were, how un-feeling, when everything below them was so mixed up. And then I envied their coolness. "Those stars have it right," I said to no one in particular. "Calm and shining. Why is it people have to be in a tussle all the time? Why isn't everyone a calm and shin-ing star?"

"We ain't fixed in one place like they are," Shorty said.

"Stars ain't fixed. They're on the move all night," Jack said.

"Them stars is so fixed that sailors on the ocean chart their course by 'em. It's us that's on the move. Those old stars stay put as we whirl by them. We're born to be restless, and where there's restlessness, there's going to be a tussle." Shorty was silent for a time, and then said, "You know, for five years, I been fixed. Maybe that's too long. Maybe it's time to get restless again."

"What do you mean?" I said.

"I'm thinkin' maybe I'll have a better chance on the railroad. What's say, Jack, you wanna work the rails?"

"Naw, what do I know about trains? Always be work for an old cowpuncher somewheres."

Shorty said, "Maybe I'll be one of them porters. Won't like the work as well, but pay's better. Maybe I could work my way up there. I could take Emma to Wichita, settle there."

"But you're the best cowboy around," I said.

"Man can't live just dreamin'. Got to grow up sometime."

His words echoed mine to Evie. Suddenly they sounded hollow.

"If I was to tell Parsons I don't want the job, he'd have to hire you, Shorty. He'd see it would work out," I said.

"Naw, because it wouldn't work out. He's right, folks don't want to see a colored man boss an outfit."

"Maybe the reason people aren't fixed like stars is so people can change their positions."

"I need to change my position," Jack said. "My hindquarters've done gone numb."

"Change their minds," I said. "What do we do?"

Jack pulled out his pistol, aimed it into the night sky, and fired one shot after another. "We get them stars to change positions." He laughed, and fired again.

Townspeople began coming out of their doors, yelling angrily. Shorty and I said good-bye to Jack and mounted up, leaving him leaning there against the stable wall. But galloping down the street, I aimed my own gun at the sky and took a shot at the stars.

27.
Truth and Evasion
Evie

Whatever was coming to me, I could take it. That's what I thought when I knew my father had seen me at the river. And I could have taken anything but the look on his face. He'd never let anything best him before, but in his face now I saw defeat. And shame.

But that look didn't last long. Soon he was mad. He stood beside his muddy buggy, arms folded. "What will your mother say? Have you lost your good sense altogether?" He shook his head. Incredulity, at least, was not one of his reactions. He thought me capable of this. "Have you been out here the whole time? Have you . . . merciful heavens, have you been consorting with one of those fellows?" His face turned purple.

"No, Papa, nothing like that."

"No? How can I believe what you tell me, ever again?"

I bowed my head and said nothing. I didn't know that I could ever be truthful again. That hurt as much as anything. I felt my knees start to shake, and it wasn't because I was wet.

But Papa saw me trembling and said, "Come now, let's get you dry." He found a buggy blanket for me and put it around my shoulders. We sat down on the grass.

"None of it's true then, about the teaching?" he asked.

"I have my certificate."

"Yes, well, we saw that. There never was a job in Bluff City?"

"No."

Neither of us spoke for a while. I wasn't thinking or feeling anything in particular. I stopped trembling, but suddenly felt very tired. I just wanted to go home and sleep in my own bed.

"What were you thinking, Evelyn?" Papa said. "You weren't thinking, I'll tell you that much. I don't know what this will do to your mother. How could you deceive us?"

"I had to do this," I said.

"You most certainly did not! What if something had happened to you, did you think of that?" He stood up abruptly. "I ought to thrash you, only you're too big for it. I suppose I can trust you to ride directly home?"

"Of course," I snapped.

"You've no grounds to take any kind of tone with me, young lady!" he thundered. "Go home and tell your mother what you've done."

I was glad to go. For the most part, my father had reacted about the way I would have expected. There would be more to come from him, but I could handle any punishments. The only thing I couldn't take was his disappointment in me, and he hadn't voiced it. I'd just seen it on his face.

I didn't know what to expect from my mother. The long ride home gave me plenty of time to think about it, but I didn't want to. I tried not to think about Tom either. It was no good wondering how things would stand from here on out. I just had to see what would happen. But I knew one thing. I was sorry I'd upset everyone, but not sorry I'd done it.

Evie

The evening sun turned the sky and the long grass pink. This was my favorite time of day. The pinking time I called it, when I was small. I loved to be on my horse riding at this hour. Andromeda picked up the pace after a few miles. She knew we were headed home and was eager to get back.

My mother saw me ride into the lane, dried out by the time I arrived, but looking nothing like the schoolteacher she thought she'd sent off. She came running out, followed by Guy and Anna.

"What happened?" she cried.

I could have cried too. I'd missed being home, and couldn't stand the stricken look on her face. "I have to talk to you," I said.

"Anna, Guy, you two go draw some water for Evie and heat it. There'll be time to say hello later. Quick, now," she said, in answer to their questioning looks.

When they went in, she led me to the porch. My pony grazed untethered on the grass in the yard. "What's wrong?" she asked.

I didn't know how to start, so I just started. "I've been on roundup," I said. "All this time. I wasn't teaching at Bluff City."

She didn't say anything, but her face went white. That unnerved me more than my father's shouting had, and I buried my face in my hands.

"Are you all right? Did they hurt you?"

"I'm fine."

She didn't say anything then.

"Mama?"

She shook her head. "Does Papa know?"

"Yes."

"He went out there and found you with them? Made you come home?"

"Yes."

"Why did you do it, Evie?" She was genuinely puzzled. I could see no disappointment or anger, just bewilderment.

"I wanted to see if my cows had survived."

"Why? The cowboys could have told you that."

"I wanted to know for myself." I couldn't explain it to her.

We sat for a long time. In the kitchen the kettle sang. Anna and Guy came running. "Let's get you cleaned up," Mama said.

Later, again in the kitchen, in my own skirt and blouse, I sat drinking tea as she pounded bread dough. I offered to help, but she shook her head. "It helps me think," she said. "I can't get over the sight of you riding in wearing those men's clothes." She sprinkled more flour on the bread-board. "You know, one time I wanted to go to a dance, but my parents forbade it. They didn't hold with dancing. But this handsome Englishman would be there, and I couldn't miss it. So I sneaked out. I didn't get caught either. I would do it again too. But I feel guilty to this day, even though I married that Englishman, with their blessing." She turned to look at me squarely. "Is there a young man involved? Is it Tom?"

I was thunderstruck. "That's not why I went," I answered, truthfully and evasively.

She studied me, sighed. "Every year, since you were small, you wanted to go on roundup." She stopped there and pounded the dough, divided it into two balls, put each ball into an oiled loaf pan. "I love to bake," she said. "And cook. I love to see you all in clean clothes and fresh beds. When I was small, though, I wanted to be a teacher. I'd make my brothers and sisters sit through hours of school, and if they wouldn't play, I'd teach the cats. I never got the chance to teach. No use wondering, is it, what would have been different if I'd been a teacher before I got married?" She put the loaves on top of the oven to rise.

"You're handy in the kitchen too, Evie, and good with a needle. And smart, smart. But you've never outgrown your horse and cows, have you?"

I looked her straight in the eye. "I'd rather help run the ranch."

She sighed again. "I know." She brushed her hands on her apron and started wiping the breadboard. "I don't see why you want it."

"But I do."

"And are you sure there's no man involved?"

I could still say no and put off the consequences that were sure to follow. I took a deep breath. "I love Tom. But we're not intimate. We're not even speaking to each other." I started trembling again.

"Of course it's Tom. What a notion. Does he know your feelings for him?"

"Yes." I swallowed. How much would I have to tell? I didn't want to get him in trouble. "He didn't approve of my going on roundup. In fact, he tried to make me go home. He doesn't want me working cattle either."

"I see." She looked relieved. "Tom's got sense enough to know how things are. He's a good man, but too young, with nothing to offer you. I'll wager every rancher's daughter falls for the hired hand. It's an old story, Evie. But you'll learn it's just a fairy tale, or a notion out of a penny dreadful. Real life doesn't work that way." She put the breadboard away and began to start supper. I felt something close up in me for good.

28.
Consequences of Deception
Tom

Shorty left. Packed his gear in the bunkhouse one morning and he was gone, riding off on his horse, waving good-bye only to me. The others, at the house, weren't up yet.

Evie lived at the house full-time now. She didn't go back to school, but in the fall she was to start teaching for real, at a one-room schoolhouse near Belton. This time, she was going to teach because she had to. The family needed the money.

The loss of a fifth of his herd hadn't wiped Parsons out, but it put a huge strain on him. He sent Chester to work for the hardware store owner in town, the father of Chester's sweetheart, Lila, with his blessing, provided Chester sent home money. Chester, of course, was more than happy to go. He was the only one happy. There was a pall over the whole place. The fancy two-wheeled buggy was sold, as were half the cow ponies, some of those settees Mrs. Parsons had been so careful of, and a mahogany bedroom set. But the Morgan horses and the elegant four-wheeled carriage remained.

To save money, Parsons didn't hire new men to replace Shorty and Jack. More and more he relied on me. Part of his financial strain, though, was self-imposed. He wanted to buy a sizable chunk of the Kendricks spread.

In a rare stroke of justice, Kendricks had suffered the greatest losses from the blizzard. His cattle had blown up against the fence on the westernmost part of his land and were trapped worse than ours. Three fourths of his herd had died. He was forced to sell out, and Parsons aimed to buy his place. I was amazed that someone whose own ranch survival was questionable could be wanting more, but Parsons explained to me that survival meant kill or be killed, forgetting that the blizzard had done the killing and he was a coyote, snapping up the leavings.

He and I had a good deal of time to talk together, because he was often out working with me now. My papa would have been glad to see this comedown, but I saw Parsons's determination and skill, and was more impressed with him than I'd ever been.

But the one subject we never covered was the one I most wanted to talk about: Evie. I didn't see Evie much. She'd kept her vow not to lie to her parents anymore, and that meant not seeing me. Her parents had been shocked by the extent of her deception more than anything, and they hadn't learned all of it. I could see that they blamed themselves for being too free with her—maybe that was why they didn't want me around. They forbade her pony rides and everything resembling ranch work. This was hard on her. When I'd see her throwing out the dishwater or taking the scraps to the dogs, I could see that she'd grown thinner, and she moved in a listless, mechanical way.

Her parents relaxed some over the summer, oddly enough, as Evie's hair grew back. I heard Mrs. Parsons laugh more, and wondered if she and Mr. Parsons thought Evie was becoming more like her old self, that the roundup was just a "youthful indiscretion." But they still didn't go to town as a family—Mr. Parsons was the only one who ever rode in, and then only when necessary. They often sent me in instead.

When Evie's story got back to town, as stories will, it caused quite a stir. I felt bad when the men talked about Evie around the counters of the stores. They tried to include me in their joking, implying that all of us cowhands must have had a good time with her, but I made it clear to them that nothing improper had gone on. I used my fists for emphasis on one occasion, and that appeared to straighten the matter out from then on.

I wasn't angry with Evie anymore. I was angry at the people who didn't understand her. To be fair, most folks admired her independence and enjoyed the joke on Parsons. But they all seemed small now, all of them people who only saw what they wanted to see. They hadn't seen how happy she was out on the range.

I knew she wouldn't change. She was biding her time, fighting to stay the same Evie while everyone around her wanted her to become different. I guessed that her emptiness was only an outward show; she was full inwardly, while I was full of business on the outside and empty inside.

I still wanted to save up enough money to buy a place. I had my eye on a parcel of the Kendricks property, because it was close to Parsons and also because it was good farmland, a wheat field and a potato field. But how could I convince Evie to be part of this?

29.
Hanging on the Vine
Evie

Riley Kendricks was back and looking for a job. He was in Papa's study one afternoon, the only person to apply for cowhand that ever entered and left by the front door. But Riley didn't stay long.

"Did you hire him?" I asked Papa. Talking with Papa and Mama had become comfortable again, maybe because they thought they were sure of me once more. I'd learned how to be careful.

Papa shook his head. "We need the help, surely, and I hate to see him suffer, but we can't afford it. He brought it on himself, though, running off to prospect. I wonder what he'll find to do around here?"

We weren't long in learning.

A few evenings later he came calling, again at the front door. He asked Mama, "Would you mind if Miss Evie took the air on the front porch with me?"

The hesitation in my mama's voice surprised me as she politely answered, "I don't see why not." I was listening hard in the kitchen as I washed dishes with Anna. Mama came in, but didn't hurry me along or fuss over me to get out there with him. I would just as soon have done dishes as talk to Riley, but I was curious and it had been two months since I'd talked to anyone my own age. I hadn't left the farm, hadn't spoken to Tom, and no one had been by to see me, until now.

Riley looked thin and not as cocksure as the last time I'd seen him, at New Year's when I'd wanted to slap him. There was a ragged edge to him, cut by six months of uncertainty.

But he hadn't grown more polite. "I heard about what you did," he sneered. "Running off on roundup with all those cowboys, dressing like a man. Plumb strange, if you ask me."

"Which nobody did," I pointed out. I got up. Lonely or not, I wouldn't sit here and take his stings. I hadn't heard what folks were saying about me, but I could guess. What business was it of theirs anyway?

"Some folks would think you'll be left hangin' on the vine for sure now. They'd think you are too wild to be fit to marry," he said.

I paused at the door, stunned. "Some folks shouldn't try to think. They're not equipped," I retorted.

"Well, you can smart off all you want. I just know what I'm telling you."

"I believe that."

"What?" He was puzzled.

"That's all you know."

"Listen here, you should just feel lucky I don't pay them no attention."

"What do you mean?" He was angling toward something I was sure I wanted no part of.

"I mean, you and me have been supposed to marry each other since we were small. I mean what you've done don't change things."

"Not like, say, running off to Colorado would?"

"I came back, didn't I?"

"Only because you're broke. Besides, our parents were the only ones who wanted us to marry."

"Well, what if I want it now?"

"You're insane," I whispered, half afraid. What if Mama and Papa thought, as Riley did, that there was danger of my never marrying, after what I'd done? Always ready before, they'd be only too happy to snap up his offer now.

"Just think about it."

"You'd better go."

As I stepped inside, the door to the kitchen swung shut. I sat at the parlor window, feeling sick. I'd thought I'd wriggle free of the marriage trap my parents set, but it had never sprung so close before. The reality of it was riding down my very lane.

Another rider rode up the lane as Riley rode off. It was Tom, looking like he had the first day I saw him ride up, when he first came. I turned away, fighting tears.

Three days after Riley's visit, Papa made a pronouncement as he passed the gravy at supper. "Evie, tell the Kendricks boy not to come around here anymore." I dropped my fork.

"What?"

"You don't care for him, do you?" Mama said.

"No, not a bit."

"It's not right to let him think he has a chance with you, then," Mama said. "We must put a stop to talk that he's going to marry you and end his family's troubles."

"He's not even looked for work lately." Papa thumped a salt shaker on the table to show his disgust. "We need to clear up a misunderstanding. No one will marry my daughter for her money— what there is of it."

I was floored, flummoxed. "Don't worry, I'll be quite clear," I said. Suddenly, my supper tasted good.

And when Riley came back a third time, I wasted no time telling him to go to blazes.

"You've just made the biggest mistake of your life. You're going to be a dried-up old maid," Riley said.

This brought Papa out on the porch. "See here, you impertinent tramp. If she never married, she'd be better off than marrying you," he said, his voice thundering.

"You're all hypocrites. I was good enough for her when my family had money."

"You've never been good enough. You've proven that," Papa retorted.

We stood together, and Mama joined us, watching Riley gallop away. Papa said, "Nonsense. All nonsense. Who wouldn't marry you, in a few

years?" But his shoulders sagged. He didn't believe it was nonsense.

I walked out to the barn. Nobody tried to stop
me. I dipped up a pail of oats for Andromeda,
scratched her neck as she ate them, but didn't try
to ride.

What was in store for me? I tried to imagine a
future now, but there didn't seem much possibility.
With no Riley, nor any other "suitable" fellow to
rebel against, I should have been happy, but I was
scared. Girls like me were supposed to marry, and
even though I hadn't wanted to be forced, there
was security in the thought. My herd would take a
long time to rebuild. What would my security be
until then? Would I be left hanging, as Riley pre-
dicted?

I'd never cared before—I'd scorned marriage.
Until Tom came along.

Drat him anyway, for pushing me out of my
scorn, making me care. And now, leaving me open
to the hurt of being without him.

30.
A Shot at the Stars
Tom

Mr. Parsons and I drove the wagon out with Belle and the Kendrickses' horse to take the fence down in June. Kendricks had agreed that it should come down, and Mr. Parsons, because of his interest in buying the spread, had offered to help. The day was hot. At the Chikaskia, the wagon had an easy time crossing a foot-wide muddy flow in the dry riverbed's center, a far cry from the swollen torrent a few months earlier. The spring flood had redesigned the river, carving the banks higher, eroding rangeland.

"Rivers and creeks on the prairie aren't predetermined," Mr. Parsons said as we rode along.

"They change course as needed. Reshape the land, carry it with them. Have you heard of the steamboat that wrecked on a snag in the Missouri thirty years ago, near Kansas City? The river changed course, over time, and left the wreck miles behind, buried in a field." He paused. "I was on that steamboat. Sixteen years old, fresh from England. My brother and I were headed out west. Of course we survived, everyone did. But one learns that change is inevitable, and one must adjust." He said no more as we rode.

When we came to the fence, he halted the team and surveyed the length of the steel strands. At last he said, "Fences are the coming thing, whether we like them or not. It would be a shame to waste all this barbed wire."

"We could always sell the barbed wire."

He shook his head. "We'll leave it."

"But what'll that do to your ranching?"

"Force me to change, no doubt." He studied the line of the fence as it disappeared north over the rim of grass. "The northernmost part of this fence adjoins that parcel you've been eyeing, does it not? A fence might be good to have when you acquire the property."

He jumped down and strode off, pretending to inspect the fenceposts. I sat there in the wagon as my heart rose up through my chest and about took off.

One afternoon, Papa came riding over the prairie, looking thin but well, although a little ridiculous on our big plow horse. He nodded to me as he dismounted and said, "Can't stay long. There somewhere we can talk?"

I led him to the bunkhouse and he tethered the bay. We pulled chairs outside because of the heat and sat by the door.

"Two things," he began. "First off, we got a letter from Caleb. He's in Wyoming, working on a ranch, and he ain't coming back."

After roundup I'd ridden to my folks' place and told them Caleb had never showed up. I hadn't told them more than that. I nodded in sympathy.

"Second thing, your sister in Virginia wrote to me. Asked after you, said she hadn't heard from you for a while. Here, read the letter." He thrust a folded sheet of paper at me.

Becky wrote that she couldn't understand why I hadn't come to my grandparents' funerals, and she didn't know why she hadn't heard from me.

Was I well? Did she need to come visit? She wanted me to return to Virginia for a while, on business. My grandparents' will had been through probate at court, and there was an inheritance of a thousand dollars to give me, as well as a decision to make about keeping or selling their property.

I read the last line again. The flat, businesslike sentence couldn't possibly carry the life-changing news it did: *There is a small inheritance of $1,000 for you.* Small to whom? A thousand dollars solved all my problems. It would set Evie and me up in our own place.

Would have. Past tense. The thought hit me like a blow.

Riley Kendricks had been out to the ranch three times now. There was no more Evie and me.

"I'll write to Becky," I told my father. I didn't want him involved in this. If he would take a hundred from me, he'd take a thousand. But he surprised me. He opened his wallet and pulled out five shining twenty-dollar gold pieces.

"If you have to go back," was all he said. I didn't need to know any more.

Now I would have something to offer. I could be one of those "suitable" fellows the Parsonses prized. And I didn't want to be. I would not mention the inheritance to them. They could take me for myself or not at all.

I had to tell Evie, though.

Evie had lately taken over the chore of gathering eggs at dusk. The evening of my father's visit, I stood in the shadows beside the water trough and waited. I almost didn't recognize her as she walked toward me carrying the egg basket. She kind of drifted, absent, like the ghost of the woman who drowned in the trough.

She didn't act surprised to see me. She didn't show anything at all.

"Stop a minute," I said, and she put down the egg basket. She folded her arms.

I'd thought of various things to say—"I can't let you go like this," or "Is there still a chance for us?"—but what came out of my mouth was possibly the stupidest: "Don't marry Riley."

She looked away. Her voice shook as she said, "I'm not marrying Riley."

Relief flooded through me. And then anxiety. With Riley out of the way, I had to face up to the real trouble. I didn't know how to tell her what I'd been thinking lately, since coming home from the roundup.

"Marry me, then."

She looked at the ground and spoke unsteadily. "I'm going to teach. Save money to buy my own place, build my own herd."

I looked away. Shadows lengthened on the grass, darkened the water in the trough. I cleared my throat.

"Evie, I have money."

"What?"

"I inherited a thousand dollars from my grand-parents in Virginia. We can buy a place together."

She looked at me then as if she saw me. "I'm glad you can have your place, Tom. I know it's what you wanted, and I'm happy for you. It doesn't change things for us."

My heart felt like it was going to fall out of my chest. She bent down to pick up the basket.

"I'm foreman now, Evie."

"So I heard. Congratulations." She turned to leave. I grabbed her arm.

"I shouldn't be, you know. Shorty should have gotten the job. But he couldn't have it because he's colored. That's not right."

"No." She tried to pull away. "I don't blame him for leaving."

"Listen. Evie, since then I've been thinking . . . I mean, over the summer. . . . Look here. Have you heard about the steamboat on the Missouri that wrecked on a snag and sank? The river's course shifted over time and the wreck ended up buried in a field."

She stopped struggling. "I've heard that story. It's my father's."

"Well, maybe folks in this world have to make shifts, to keep up with the river."

"What do you mean?"

"I mean I don't know why you want to ranch, but I know that you do. That ought to be good enough for me. Of course it is. Evie, I'm all empty inside."

She set the basket down and faced me. I put my arms around her, pressed my forehead to hers.

"What do I do?" I whispered. "I took a gun and fired at the stars, but they didn't change."

"What'd you do that for?"

"Maybe I was trying to move what was fixed. Maybe I've shifted a bit. I want you to be happy so we can be happy. What do I do?"

She laughed then, almost a sob. "Don't go firing any more guns," she said, and then she pulled me close. Her breath was soft against my ear as she said, "But wanting both of us to be happy, now that's a good start."

I carried the egg basket for her as we turned to walk to the house. At the back door, she paused on the steps. "Why don't you come in?" she asked.

And so I did.

Author's Note

Like its predecessor, *Grasslands*, this is a might-have-been story based on some of the events and attitudes of the time period. These books helped me reimagine Kansas in the 1880s:

An Army of Women, by Michael Lewis Goldberg. Baltimore, Md.: Johns Hopkins University Press, 1997.

Cowboys and Cattleland, by H. H. Halsell. Originally published 1937; reprinted by Texas Christian University Press. Fort Worth, Tex.: Texas Christian University Press, 1983.

Cowgirls: Women of the American West, by Teresa Jordan. Lincoln, Nebr.: University of Nebraska Press, 1992.

Kansas: The History of the Sunflower State, 1854–2000, by Craig Miner. Lawrence, Kans.: University of Kansas Press, 2002.

The Women's West, edited by Susan Armitage and Elizabeth Jameson. Norman, Okla.: University of Oklahoma Press, 1987.

The lines of poetry Tom recites at Christmas Eve are from "The Eve of St. Agnes," by John Keats. The lines of Shorty's song are from an old Christmas carol, found in *Christmas in the Big House, Christmas in the Quarters,*

Author's Note

by Patricia C. McKissack and Fredrick L. McKissack (New York: Scholastic, 1994).

The blizzard of 1886 killed an estimated 25,000 cattle across western Kansas. There were heavy snowfalls throughout that winter.

Kansas women got the right to vote in municipal elections in 1887 and elected the first female mayor in the country, Mrs. Susanna Salter of Argonia.